Time Killer
Mike Boylan

Copyright © 2008 by Mike Boylan

All rights reserved

ISBN: 978-0-6152-1992-9

This is a work of fiction. Names. characters, places, and incidents are either the product mof the author's imagination or are used fictitiously. Any resemblance to actual events or locales or persons, living or dead, is coincidental.

To my wife Sabine, who never doubted I would finish.

Author's Note

This novel was written as part of the NaNoWriMo project.

Each November, hundreds of thousands of people set out to write a 50,000 word novel in 30 days. The project starts Nov. 1 and ends Nov. 30. If you have 50,000 words by the end of the month, you win.

What do you win? A sense of accomplishment. That and a nickel will buy you a piece of Bazooka Joe bubble gum, but the pride in finishing a novel is actually priceless.

As I write this note, months after finishing "Time Killer" and weeks before sending it off to a self-publishing web site to unleash upon the world, I am staring at a huge Ikea bookshelf crammed with novels - some good, others great and a few that are just kick-your-ass amazing. Soon, my novel will be on one of those shelves and that is just mind-blowing.

I've been writing creatively since middle school and still I never dreamed that I would ever write a novel. It wasn't a goal of mine, despite how in love with the written word I am. I figured I would always be a novel reader and never a novel writer and then I found this contest. Now, I am a novelist. That can be a part of my resume and I can nonchalantly drop this fact in conversations at cocktail parties (which is a big plus), but it means much more to me on an individual and private basis.

Finishing "Time Killer" means that I saw something through to the end. Aside from not being physically exerting, I imagine novel writing is just like running a marathon. I started fast and then started to hit those long stretches where I wasn't sure I would be able to finish. Metaphorically speaking, my legs buckled a few times and I had to splash some water on my face to keep going.

Hopefully, it won't be easy to spot when I hit those patches while you are reading this book.

"Time Killer" isn't the great American novel. I know this. The few people who took a look at it during its editing stage after November commented that it was a good read and, more importantly, a fun read. I hope you find it to be entertaining and I am glad that you are here and are about to settle in to this book. I won't keep you much longer. I just want to thank you for supporting me and my first novel. I think I have many more in me and I know that each one will get better and better.

I plan on participating in NaNoWriMo every year, but now I think I can write a novel without the time constraints too.

So, good reading to you,

Mike

Chapter 1

I have seen where the wolf has slept by the silver stream.
I can tell by the mark he left you were in his dream
Ah child of countless trees, ah child of boundless seas.

"Cassidy"- Grateful Dead

Halloween fell on a Friday this year and Marcia Danville fell on a Saturday. She had left her home early that morning, as the lawns of her neighbors appeared to steam clean themselves from the trampling the night before, and headed for the track of the local high school. Marcia walked 16 laps around the track from September through May, allowing her to eat whatever her little heart desired. She did not understand the women who allowed themselves to graze and grow like cattle, nor did she understand the ones who starved themselves to look like emaciated ghouls. According to Marcia, a little bit of exercise and not gorging oneself on gallons of ice cream when a small bowl would do just fine was all one had to do.

She wound her way around the corner at the top of her street and hung a left towards Cabot High School.

On quiet mornings, such as this, Marcia felt good about living in the small, Massachusetts town of Cabot for her entire life. She knew her neighbors and their families, some of them dating back over 30 some odd years to when she was a student at the very same school she walked towards today. The roads, which were busy Monday through Friday at nearly all hours, were quiet Saturday mornings and even quieter on Sunday mornings, but Marcia didn't walk on the Lord's Day. It gave her a chance to reflect on her week, the weekend which still lay ahead, and what the following work week would look like. Marcia was a few years away from retirement. Well, more than a few, although she still clung to the hope that her husband, Gary, would insist that she retire at the same time as him, which was three short years away.

Marcia worked at the Shepard Senior Center, a high-rise apartment for seniors of varying capacities. She liked the work, or at least she used to, but as she got older, the work got harder and certainly more depressing. In the last year, three women who used to be church colleagues of Marcia's had moved in to Shepard. Fran Hampton was still sharp as a tack and just lived there for convenience, but Billie Jessup and Marie Rogers were shells of their former selves and withdrawing more every day. These women were all 10 years Marcia's senior, at least, but facing her mortality every day had started to weigh on her.

Marcia crossed over two side streets and could see the high school football field in the distance. She gasped as she saw the goalposts on the football field draped in toilet paper. With each step, she could see more of the vandalism at the school. There were foul words written in spray paint on the field, in the end zone and in bright yellow on the doors leading to the gym. In addition to the "f-bombs" and the slurs about Cabot's rising black population, Marcia saw the phrase "More to Cum!" written in giant, red letters with the artist apparently "sleeping it off" right nearby.

She drew her cell phone out of her pocket like a sheriff in an old Western, ready to dial the police. Marcia could not see the point of vandalism. Sure, in her teen years, she had rolled one or two of trees downtown with toilet paper following a Cabot High

School football win, but she couldn't make heads or tails of the graffiti she constantly saw on train rides into Boston. Nonsensical, spray painted markings that lined the walls of the back of every building and abandoned railroad car from one town to the next. And now her alma mater was once again emblazoned with profanity and racist remarks.

Marcia was angry, or rather really "P-O'ed," which is something she picked up from Gary when he talked about a bunch of the young electricians he worked with. She had enjoyed seeing the little ones out trick or treating the night before and had gladly placed Dum-Dum lollipops in their shopping bags and pillowcases, but now she saw the true aftermath of the holiday. Those little cowboys and princesses grew up to be teenagers, passed out in their own vomit, amidst their heinous displays of mischief and monkeyshines.

Early in her marriage to Gary, Cabot and some of the neighboring towns had to contend with some extremely violent Halloweens. The teenagers at the time, fueled mostly on rotgut whiskey and anger at their poor prospects for a happy life, called Halloween Devil's Night. These hoodlums didn't just smash the occasional pumpkin or soap the windows of cars. Oh no, some of these kids started fires. They burned down an abandoned Fotomat in the parking lot of the Shop Well and one nasty little scumbag named Dickie Grant set fire to what he thought was a homeless man, but was really a Shepard patient with Alzheimer's who had wandered off the grounds. Devil's Night cooled down quite a bit after that, thank God, but that one year of arson, rage and murder, had soured Marcia on the holiday for many years. She had only started turning her lights on again on Halloween night a few years back and it was only this year that she had felt comfortable to sit on the porch and watch the parades of happy children.

And she had enjoyed herself, last night, but the scene at the high school brought Devil's Night back, leaving it stinging and hot at the back of her throat.

She resolved that she would call the police. Oh yes, Chief Woodfin would definitely hear about this and get to personally escort this crumpled strumpet or hung-over horndog home, but not before Mrs. Marcia Danville got her words in first. Marcia picked up her pace and crossed the street to the school's parking lot. She jogged down the hill until she reached the edge of the athletic fields and stopped to unzip her sweatshirt a little ways to cool off a bit. From this angle, the offending words on the field were not visible, but the toilet paper shifted with the breeze, with some of it occasionally sticking to poles due to moisture.

Wake up, you little shit, thought Marcia. *I dare you to wake up and see me coming. I want to see the fear and shame in your eyes as I get up in your face.*

Marcia continued to rant in her mind as she neared the target of her rage. *This doesn't happen here and believe you me, it won't happen again. This is a nice town and pieces of garbage are dealt with. You can do whatever you like down on Bennett Street, most people do, on the train tracks or behind the bowling alley, but you leave the school and the football field alone.*

Marcia was boiling over when she reached the body and what she had meant to be a solid tap from her pink and green lined Nike Air Pegasus sneakers was more of a kick. The force behind the kick was enough to roll the body over, which prompted Marcia to realize that this was no drunken teenybopper getting her ratty, navy blue Abercrombie sweatshirt muddy, this was a dead and horribly mutilated body.

Marcia almost certainly screamed, but it didn't last long enough for any of the neighbors of the school to hear. She fainted at the sight of the poor girl below her and was in a semi-catatonic state of shock when Ellie Clark, another lap-walker, found her 35 minutes later.

Within minutes of Ellie Clark's discovery of the passed out older woman and the murdered teen, the parking lot of the high school was filled with police cars, a crime scene unit van, ambulances, a fire truck and cars of interested passers-by. Ned Kopp, the principal of Cabot High School, stood silently on the edge of the football field, away from the on-lookers and watched the members of the public safety teams doing their jobs. Kopp had been called by the police after they discovered that no one at the scene could identify the body. He could. He knew it was Cassidy Samuels, one of many average students who tend to float through their four years with nothing remarkable occurring. Kopp teared up at the thought that something remarkable had in fact happened to Cassidy.

He watched the EMTs helping Marcia Danville to her feet and gingerly walking her back to the parking lot, her face ensconced behind an oxygen mask, and he watched as police officers and detectives swarmed around Cassidy's body. One man took pictures of her gruesome stab wounds, holes that Kopp had inadvertently seen before retreating to the safety of the perimeter of the crime scene. *His school was now a crime scene. Crime Scene High.*

Cassidy had been stabbed repeatedly and the murderer had ripped and torn at the girl's stomach and around her pelvis and vagina. It looked like a very poor attempt at carving her like a pumpkin, as if the person wielding the blade made jagged mountain shapes in her flesh, trying to create eyes or a creepy smile. Kopp hysterically screamed the word murderer in his head, sure that he was beginning to crack up under the pressure and the knowledge that when school started again on Monday thousands of students would look to him for guidance. All while the MURDERER would likely be gazing up at him in the assembly he would have to call to relay the terrible news or listening to him over the intercom with a smirk on his face.

It had to be a guy, didn't it? A girl couldn't possibly commit a crime like this, Kopp wondered, answering his question by acknowledging that he knew plenty of mean-spirited, violent girls roamed his halls.

Cassidy's black skirt (she had been dressed as a sexy witch) had been sliced at and her underwear had been split. Though Kopp, thankfully, did not notice, it did not escape the attention of the police that Cassidy had likely been raped. Detective Christopher Leonard had noticed everything. It was his first murder investigation, the first in Cabot in 28 years, and it had his adrenaline pumping. The whole morning had been crystal clear for Leonard and he felt as if his eyesight was better than perfect.

He pointed out traces of semen in Cassidy's powder blue panties and asked Bob Hannah, a CSI technician, to get samples of the stuff beneath her fingernails. He noticed Cassidy's black right eye, the remnants of red under her left nostril, suggesting a bloody nose that hadn't been running for hours now, and a split lip. He also noticed a hickey, the term he put on his report was "love bite" next to smudges of her dirt on both sides of her neck and just above her left breast. Leonard also noticed that unlike every other teenage girl in Cabot, Cassidy wasn't packing a cell-phone or a purse. Her killer had likely taken them, hoping that their absence would take longer to identify the girl, and had probably ditched them in the woods somewhere or a trash can at a nearby shopping plaza, anything to throw the cops off the case.

Leonard wasn't worried. He had always been told that murder cases often had the simplest solutions. If you found a married woman dead, the killer was probably her husband. So, if you found a dead teenage girl at the 50-yard line of the high school football field, the murderer could probably be a scared, angry, teenage football player. He supposed that it could also be a disgruntled coach or faculty member or some random pervert who stumbled across some easy prey last night. Thinking about it now, murder cases involving teens couldn't have a simple solution.

It doesn't matter, he thought, there was probably enough DNA evidence here to clone a copy of the killer, if he had to, so he just stood a few feet away from Cassidy's pale, and growing paler, corpse and noticed everything, including the arrival of what passed for Cabot's media, Ken O'Donnell, the news reporter for the Cabot Clarion, the town's oldest and only newspaper.

O'Donnell screeched his beige Dodge minivan to a halt in the lower parking lot of the high school and stormed out of the vehicle, practically running to the gathering around the body. The camera around his neck swung back and forth wildly.

"Get the hell out of here, Kenny," Leonard growled at him and several of the officers around glanced back at Leonard, unaware the fresh faced detective could ever sound that intimidating. "We'll have a conference later today or tomorrow and we'll be sure to invite you."

"Chris -"

"It's Detective Leonard," roared Leonard. He thought he could see piss running down O'Donnell's legs, but the reporter was undaunted.

"Detective Leonard, this is the first murder in Cabot in, I don't know how many years, it's big news. Give me something," O'Donnell pleaded.

"I can't. We haven't been able to notify next of kin yet, so you'll have to wait. Now, get back behind the yellow tape with all of the other rubber neckers. When we can tell you something, we will."

Ken O'Donnell snapped three quick shots of the huddle around the body, a female from what he could tell, and skulked away. Typically, he got along great with the local police and got everything he needed, but now that there was a murder in town, it was going to be a pissing contest and the cops, especially Leonard, were out to win.

As O'Donnell ducked under the stretched police tape boundary and began walking back to his car, his cell phone rang. His ring tone, "Hair of the Dog" by Nazareth, with the oh so polite chorus of "Now you're messing with a son of a bitch," caused a bit of a stir among the gawkers, who felt that O'Donnell's cell phone was just plain rude. It ruined the solemnity of their respectful staring. The ring let O'Donnell know that his boss, Jerry Jackson, was on the other end of the phone.

The minute O'Donnell flipped open the phone, he could hear Jerry barking.

"What's this about a murder?"

"I'm at the high school right now, Jerry. There's a dead girl on the 50 yard line."

"Who?"

"I don't know," O'Donnell said, rubbing the spot where the bridge of his nose met his forehead. Ken had felt fine all morning, but now a headache started to nag at the front of his brain. "Leonard won't tell me anything. Apparently, they haven't been able to contact her next of kin yet."

"Got any ideas?"

"Sorry, I stopped knowing who the pretty high school girls were about 20 years ago." He may not know who they were, but he did find himself staring from time to time when he had to cover a big game. There was no harm in looking and most of the girls, from the cheerleaders to the hyperactive gossips running around texting their friends on the sidelines, had a fresh quality that Ken had to admit he still found alluring. He loved his wife and his family, but these girls brought back memories of kisses that tasted like fruit and the palpable excitement at touching skin against skin.

"Find out who she is," Jerry ordered.

"It won't do me any good. I can't print it until they tell me who she is, unless I never want a cop to call me back ever again."

Jerry Jackson fumed on the other end of the line. O'Donnell might be right, hell, of course, he was right, but what Jackson had wanted him to say was, 'I'm on it.' That's all. Just a little white lie to make Jackson believe that his ace news reporter was doing something other than hanging around a parking lot with a thumb up his ass.

"Kenny, this is the first murder in our town in over 20 years," Jackson said, shifting his tone to try to calm his reporter. "In about one hour, the TV news crews and reporters from the major newspapers are going to descend on this town and you will be the smallest fish in the smallest pond. You need to open your mind and think of every angle you can, so that we have the freshest news, first."

There was a pause where neither man spoke. Jerry picked up his coffee mug with a smiley face on it and sipped the dark brew inside, while Ken watched an EMT vomit several feet away from the girl's corpse.

"Do you understand me, Ken? We have got minutes here to get something on our web site and start leading the way on this thing."

"Yeah. I'm on it."

Ken hung up and Jerry smiled. Good boy, he thought.

Jerry's paper, The Cabot Clarion, had been around for 97 years. It was founded by Herbert Balch, who had also served as the town's librarian and historian. The Clarion had started out as a weekly newspaper and remained such until Balch passed away in 1949. After his death, the paper, now under the control of Balch's nephew, Ed Reynolds, went daily for a three year period before Reynolds sold the paper in an attempt to pay off a massive amount of gambling debts. David Westerley purchased the paper next, getting what everyone in town considered a sweetheart of a deal, and pushed the publication days back to three days a week; Tuesday, Thursday and Saturday. This allowed Westerley to enjoy long weekends at his lake home in New Hampshire, sometimes with his family and other times with an assortment of both male and female friends. As Westerley grew older and salacious tales of his alleged escapades grew more infrequent, he grew closer to his paper and a key member of his staff, Lenox Jackson, an import from the south. Lenox started out as an editorial assistant but had worked his way up to Westerley's most trusted news man. Westerley retired in the early 1980s and handed the keys of the paper to Jackson, now a top notch reporter and quite the shrewd businessman. Jackson grew the paper to its current incarnation, a daily newspaper that provided up to the minute news of every political event, school function and sport played in the town of Cabot and several surrounding municipalities. The staff swelled to record numbers and tons of news filled every page.

When the internet came into play, Jackson, prodded by his son, Jeremiah (Jerry), bought in hook, line and sinker and created a web site that rivaled that of most major newspapers. It was fast, easy to maneuver around and, again, chock full of information. Lenox Jackson retired soon after the millennium and left his son in charge as the newspaper industry hit a major slowdown. The major newspapers were jettisoning top tier talent and salaries and advertisers slunk away from putting ads in print. Small town newspapers were immune in some respects - the big boys were never going to cover girls field hockey or planning commission meetings - but advertisers were squeamish about sinking a lot of money into dinosaurs like newspapers and even more squeamish about putting money in something unknown like the internet. Jerry had to make some tough decisions and the easiest one to make was to shrink the staff. Twenty five staff writers became 10 and those still receiving a paycheck were expected to update the web site continually, shoot pictures at every event they attended and even get video at some of these same events.

Today, the Cabot Clarion was a successful publication with an award winning web site. Jerry Jackson should have felt on top of the world, proud that he was continuing the newspaper's proud tradition as it neared its 100th anniversary, but the truth was, until the murder, he was bored. To an outsider who flips through the newspaper occasionally, the news seems fresh and interesting, but the people on the inside know it is a stale, smelly beast. Looking at years and years of stories side by side, the plots repeat themselves almost in the same times and places every year. The characters may change, but the quotes are always the same and not even the best reporters in the world, of which Jerry did not have the pleasure of employing any, could do much to make the same old stories fun and interesting.

Outside of Jerry, the Cabot Clarion employed six people: Nancy Frangelli, the receptionist/payroll/classifieds person, Susan Weiner, the ad sales manager for all Clarion Publications, Derek Masters, the graphics and web guru, Hillary Ames, the features reporter/fluff writer, Sam Vollmer, the kid who covered sports for four of the six Clarion papers, and Ken, the news reporter and all around utility guy. It was bare bones, but the team was solid. They got the paper out on time, made few mistakes and all earned what Jerry considered to be the appropriate salary, namely a little less than they probably deserved.

Jerry was feeling a little maudlin as he poured his third cup of coffee and woke his laptop up from its screen saving slumber. His wife and daughter were out for a girls day at the spa, so he was left alone with his thoughts of growing up, and never out, of the news business. The news was rarely good and this ironically tended to be good for business. Take today's murder for example. Kenny would be writing on this for the next 12-14 months with stories about the investigation, the capture of the killer, the court case, the aftermath, features on the victim, the people who knew, or thought they knew, the killer, what the experts say, ways to keep yourself safe from a killer's attack, the other murders in Cabot history (all 12 of them) and the list went on and on.

As a father though, Jerry did not want to think about and couldn't stomach thinking about his daughter being mangled by some maniac and left on the middle of a football field. Anna was 20 years old now, hopefully nearing the age where she would finally leave the nest and make her mark on the world, and yet he just wanted to keep her close and in his arms. Like most fathers, Jerry sat gazing off into the distance recapping the last 20 years in his head.

He was startled out of his memories by the ringing of the telephone some time later.

"I've got enough for a story," Ken said, before Jerry could even say 'Hello.' "It's on the web now and I'll add to it after the press conference tomorrow."

"Who was she?" Jerry asked.

"A junior at the high school named Cassidy Samuels," reported Ken. "She was in the school chorus, and that's about all we know right now. I'll talk with her family and classmates on Monday morning, but right now I just want to go home and hug my kids."

"Yeah," Jerry said, hanging up the phone. He jostled his computer awake and went looking for O'Donnell's story.

Chapter 2

Well bad news travels like wild fire, good news travels slow
They all call me Wildfire ha ha, cause everybody knows
I'm bad news everywhere I go

"Bad News" - Johnny Cash

Town rocked by gruesome Halloween murder
By Ken O'Donnell
kodonnell@cabotclarion.com

"It was an evil act committed by a monster from hell."

Those were the words spoken through choking sobs from the mother of Cabot's first murder victim in over 20 years, as police officers led her away from identifying the body at the local morgue.

Cassidy Samuels, a junior at Cabot High School and member of the school's chorus, was found dead on the 50-yard line of the high school's football field Saturday morning. Her body was discovered by local resident Marcia Danville who fainted at the sight of Samuels mutilated corpse.

The Cabot Police Department are still searching for a motive for the murder and a suspect.

"We are conducting a full-scale investigation and welcome any information that people can give us about Cassidy's whereabouts on Friday night," said Detective Chris Leonard, the lead investigator on the case. "If you saw her at a Halloween party or out trick or treating, please let us know so we can establish a timeline of events."

The Cabot police are currently being assisted by members of neighboring police departments, but Mayor Pauline Krasnick would not rule out asking for assistance from the state police or federal authorities.

"I have absolute faith in the capabilities of our local police department," Krasnick said. "But we don't have a lot of experience with investigating murders and we need to apprehend the culprit and make sure this doesn't happen again. The window of opportunity to find evidence or solid leads is closing by the minute."

Makeshift memorials for Samuels have been installed in and around the football field and the First Baptist Church of Cabot has organized a candlelight vigil scheduled to walk the track around the football field tonight starting at dusk.

"We just want Cassidy to know that we love her and will always remember her," said Geoff Lyman, the junior class president and president of the Fellowship of Christian Athletes. "I don't know how anybody could do something so horrible to someone."

Rumors have been running rampant around the school with some students theorizing that Samuels was the victim of a jealous lover, while others believe that it could only be the work of a deranged maniac on the loose and seeking more young students to prey on. Detective Leonard and the rest of the police department refuse to comment on any of the popular theories and believe that evidence will point them in the right direction.

Mayor Krasnick and the police have installed a temporary curfew of 8 p.m. for all teenagers in the town until further notice.

Who was Cassidy Samuels?
By Ken O' Donnell
kodonell@cabotclarion.com

In the official numbers from the start of the school year, Cabot High School was listed as having a student population of 957. That number is now one less after the murder of Cassidy Samuels sometime late Friday night or early Saturday morning.

Who was Cassidy Samuels though?

She was a daughter to Steven and Rebecca Samuels, a sister to younger brother, Nick, and a granddaughter to Dean and June Samuels and Walter and April Fennimore. Her parents described her as a warm and caring girl with a penchant for creative writing and illustration. They said she wanted to write children's books when she grew up and her brother, Nick, tearfully read her favorite book, Shel Silverstein's "The Giving Tree," at an impromptu gathering at the makeshift memorial at the school's football stadium, which is where Samuels' body was found Saturday morning.

Her friends in the school chorus have tied balloons to the fence and placed stuffed animals and posters with their declarations of grief around the stadium.

"Cassidy was the nicest person at our school," said Audrey Lipscomb, a sophomore who was a soprano like Cassidy. "This just doesn't make any sense."

When asked if they thought one of their peers could have committed such a horrible act, nearly every student approached said no. Yet none of the dozens of people this reporter talked to had seen Cassidy the night of the murder. "If everyone was such good friends with her, how come nobody spent any time with her on Halloween." Said an officer who asked not to be named.

The memorial service for Cassidy Samues is scheduled for this evening in the Cabot High School auditorium. The funeral will take place tomorrow morning at the Arcadia Funeral Home on Tremont Avenue at 10 a.m.

Few in town remember the last murder
By Jerry Jackson
editor@cabotclarion.com

My father hired me to cover sports for the Cabot Clarion after I graduated from UMass. It was 1980 and I knew very little about sports and even less about the newspaper. I knew a lot about Cabot though and my dad was sure that I would learn plenty about newspaper writing and the business in general soon enough.

He was right, although I wish that I didn't have to learn the things I learned that year. 1980 was the year of Cabot's last murder and it too occurred on Halloween, or what a certain band of people that year called Devil's Night. The tradition of mischief and violence had grown more and more reckless over the previous two years and in 1980 it went way too far. One very drunk teenager, Richard "Dickie" Grant, had started several fires around town. He set the teeter totter at Tanis Park ablaze, started a fire on the passenger seat of an abandoned car and then decided to set what he thought was a homeless person on fire. The victim wasn't a homeless person, but a patient of the Shepard Senior Center who had wandered off the premises that night.

My father dragged me with him everywhere he went over the course of the next few weeks and I got a baptism by fire in what a murder looks like and what it does to a town. It is an ugly, savage thing and there is always more than one victim.

Henry Jarvis burned to death near the Herrick River and his death is simply horrifying to imagine. His daughter, Denise, had to fly in from mission work in Venezuela to attempt to identify his remains. She and the rest of his family had to sit through months and months of trials and appeals until they finally got to hear the verdict of life in prison without the possibility of parole.

Grant destroyed his family, too. His mother, understandably, started to use alcohol and drugs to numb the pain of losing her only son to jail and dealing with the crushing weight of guilt she felt the town placed upon her. His siblings started to get in trouble in school and with the law and all of them ended up either in juvenile detention, jail or foster care.

Cabot was a victim, too. It was a long time before the new generation didn't have the murder imprinted on its brain and now we have a new group forced to live under another dark cloud.

That year I learned a devastating lesson of journalism, one that made me leap at the chance at getting behind the desk and staying there when the opportunity presented itself. The lesson is this - journalism is often bad news - even good news can sometimes be bad news for someone else - and a reporter must desensitize him or herself from it. They must constantly look at it, describe it completely, and yet rarely give any credence to their opinion on the matter. It is better not to think of something in any particular way at all. Try not to care either way and you are well on your way to being a good journalist.

I wept for Henry Jarvis - anyone would - but 14 months later, when the verdict was finally in on Dickie Grant - I simply walked out of the courtroom with a blank look on my face. I was glad Grant got a life sentence, but Henry Jarvis wasn't going to come back. All I really wanted was to move on to another story and leave the burned senior citizen and his broken, teenage killer locked away in an attic of my mind never to be thought of again.

And yet, as anyone in this town who lived here in 1980 will tell you, there are not many days that pass without a thought about Henry Jarvis and Devil's Night.

It was a time where we felt we had lost the town and for a time we had.

Cabot will never be the same again
an OP-ED piece from Ken O'Donnell

When Cassidy Samuels was murdered, our town and our way of life was destroyed as well. Within hours of the news spreading from house to house and neighbor to neighbor, we started to lock our car doors when we ran in to the store for a cup of coffee and we knew we would have to start locking our doors at night.

Unlike the simulated murders on television or at the movies, there is no clear suspect to point the finger at, so it points at everyone we see . We are only safe in the knowledge that we are not the murderer. Everyone else is a suspect and guilty until proven innocent.

Yes, my friends and neighbors, there is a killer at large in Cabot He is a coward in the shadows and he will undoubtedly try to strike at the weakest among us again with his only true weapon, the element of surprise. Let us turn the tables on him.

This town of warm smiles is now full of cold shoulders and mistrusting eyes. Our terror and paranoia had to be a part of the murderer's sinister plan and we must thwart his dastardly hopes. A town divided by fear is easier to attack and conquer. We must band together, stay safe and take care of each other.

Chapter 3

Something
Is about to give
I can feel it coming
I think I know what it means

"Kite" - U2

Most days at the Cabot Clarion start with Nancy Frangelli opening the doors around 8 a.m., starting a pot of Dunkin Donuts coffee, per Jerry's request, turning on the phone system and flipping through the Boston Globe. Nancy is usually the only one in the building until 9 a.m., but since the murder the staff has been keeping strange hours. It seems like an unspoken edict from Jerry let people know that things had to run tighter for the time being. By the time Nancy came in the day after the "murder edition," as Sam so crudely put it yesterday, was published, the entire staff was already cracking way on the follow-up paper.

Ken, decked out in his funeral garb, was going through pictures from the memorial service with Derek, trying to select some nominees to present to Jerry for the front page. Sam was talking with someone about whether or not school had been cancelled so that the students could attend the funeral (it had not) and Hillary was working on laying out a photo page from the memorial service and the gatherings around the Cassidy memorial with a frown on her face.

"Doesn't this seem like a bit much?" she asked no one in particular.

"No, it doesn't. It seems very appropriate," Ken responded in a clipped and snippy tone.

Hillary was ready to let it go. Ken had been working his ass off since the murder and it was better him than her. She knew that she could not handle dealing with all of the unbearably uncomfortable situations that Ken had to. The fact that he spoke with Cassidy's parents so soon after they identified her body, showed a tremendous dedication to his job. It also seemed a little callous, cold and clinical, but it had to be done. The "big boys" shouldn't be deferred to in that situation, just because they represented major publications. The local newspaper should be the one to get the story first. Theirs was the paper that would treat the murder, the loss of one of their own, with dignity and respect, not just as another murder in a paper filled with them throughout the year.

And yet, they were capitalizing on Cassidy's death too. They knew that more people were reading their paper now more than ever and they also knew that their web site was getting a higher volume of traffic than the Boston newspapers because they had more localized information. Students were leaving their messages for Cassidy on a web page dedicated to the girl, every photo that Ken had taken over the last few days found its way to galleries and every reader offered their opinion on who the killer could be, what the police could be doing better and what the people in town would do when they found the killer.

Hillary had to admit that despite how maudlin and macabre all of their murder coverage was, they were doing a good job. The entire staff had responded very well, picking up their pace and working outside of their normal beats and hours to make sure that everything involved in putting out a complete paper got done on time.

Nancy entered the editorial room with a box that had just arrived.

"You got a package, Kenny," she said, standing a few feet behind him with a cardboard box the size of a shoebox.

"Who's it from?" he asked, not bothering to turn around.

"It just says Cabot High School as the return address. The UPS guy just dropped it off," she said, about to place it on his desk and go back downstairs. She and Kenny were probably the only two people in the office who didn't get along. They had worked together the longest, but always spoke to each other very formally. Sam and Hillary had often pondered what could be in the pair's past that would make them so cold to each other. The first thought was an affair, but Nancy was Ken's senior by 20 years and outweighed the scrawny reporter by 75 pounds.

"Here, let me see it," he said in something like an order. Nancy turned around, placed it in his hands, and left the room. She muttered something under her breath, but nobody heard it or cared to comment.

Everyone stopped what they were doing for the moment and watched Ken open the box. He peeled open the box and took out an enclosed envelope that lay on top of piles of colored tissue paper.

"What is it?" Hillary asked, thinking that perhaps the school had sent him a memento for his careful and considerate reporting of the tragedy.

"I don't know-" Ken started, as he sifted through the paper before dropping the box and making a treacherous noise. It was somewhere between a moan and a scream. Hillary stood up and looked at Kenny, who was quivering and going pale. He wore a look that said he was going to throw up and he followed through on that promise very quickly. Hillary's eyes were drawn to the fingertips that Ken had placed in the box. They were marked with blood.

Did someone place razors in the bottom of the box, Hillary wondered, starting to step towards the box to take a peak.

"Don't look in there," Ken screamed, trails of spittle dripping from the corner of his mouth. "Stay away from there!"

"Wh-what is it, what's in there?" Hilary asked in a meek voice with the trace of a sob starting.

While Ken held Hillary off, Sam stood up and looked over Ken's shoulder and into the box.

"Oh Jesus! Fucking ..." Sam said, stumbling several feet away and now pressing his very clammy head on to the cool wall.

Jerry came storming down the hall, wondering what all the commotion was. Ken was now standing up and holding Hillary, shielding her from what was inside the box.

"What the hell is going on here, Ken?" he asked.

"Call the police, Jerry. We've just been contacted by the killer and we have a key piece of evidence," Ken said quietly, while Sam gagged in the corner.

Jerry couldn't resist looking in the box first and Ken did not attempt to stop him. Jerry gasped as he saw the bloody lump that lay in the pile of tissue paper, soaked red with blood and viscera. He was sure he saw several tiny fingers in the pile before his eyes teared up and he heaved up his breakfast.

The police arrived within five minutes with Detective Leonard leading the way. Two officers took the fetus away and Leonard sat down with the staff in the conference room.

"Where's this letter?" he asked.

Hillary handed it to him, while Ken just sat with his eyes looking directly at the table.

"You haven't read it yet?" Leonard asked, even though the fact that the envelope was still sealed told him that this was so. He couldn't believe they hadn't been curious enough to look at the letter. Even though they had all seen something undeniably horrible, they also had a missive from the killer in their hands. How could the "media" pass up an opportunity like this?

"It's addressed to you, Kenny," he said.

"I don't care. I fucking quit!"

Jerry looked up, shocked.

"What?"

"I can't do this anymore," Ken said, gathering strength, though his voice shuddered. "I've got a family at home, Jerry. People who count on me. I can't be playing cat and mouse with a killer."

"Ken, please reconsider, let's just .." Jerry started, but Ken interrupted him immediately.

"No. No, thank you. You've done a lot for me in my career, Jerry. You made me what I am, but I think I'm just going to move back to Pennsylvania and sell insurance with my Dad."

Everyone sat silently in the room for a minute before Leonard broke in.

"Do you mind if I read this, Ken?" he asked.

"It's yours, now."

"Wait," Jerry said. "Chris - Detective Leonard. Please let us read this before you take it in as evidence. We deserve to know if there has been a direct threat on Ken -"

"It doesn't matter, Jerry," Ken yelled. "Threat or not, this guy sent me an unborn baby. I don't feel comfortable here anymore and I really don't want to know what this guy has in store for me."

"Fine, Ken. I get it!" Jerry yelled back. "I don't blame you, but show a little bit of journalistic integrity. We have the chance to be the first people to hear directly from the murderer, so show a little backbone, open the envelope and read the letter before you hightail it out of here."

Ken reached out towards Leonard, received the letter and handed it to Jerry. He stood up and started to walk out of the room.

"I'm going to collect my things and I'll send for my last paycheck," Ken said, unable to meet anyone in the eye on his way out of the room.

At the time, everyone in the conference room, including Leonard, thought that Ken's was being a bit hasty with his resignation.

They all changed their mind after reading the letter.

Chapter 4

I'm living in an age
That calls darkness light
Though my language is dead
Still the shapes fill my head
I'm living in an age
Whose name I don't know
Though the fear keeps me moving
Still my heart beats so slow

"My Body is a Cage" - Arcade Fire

Dear Mr. O'Donnell,
  Kudos to you on being the first one with the story of my inaugural murder. We are forever linked. Your work and your words are in my scrapbook, one which I am sure to revisit time and time again.
  All along I felt it would be very important for the Cabot Clarion to be the one to break the story first. Why you ask? Well, as a Cabot resident, I always turn to my local newspaper and the web site for up to the minute breaking local news. You do such a good job.
  Feel free to use that in any future advertising your publication does.
  On a serious note though, local newspapers are the lifeblood of this great nation. Their news is the real news behind the staged and manufactured news clips and sound bites on the national stage. Plus, local papers serve as a fundamental document for the historical record and I am now a key figure in the history of the town.
  You may be shaking your head, thinking that one brutal murder does not a historical figure make, but you are wrong. I am far from done and as you continue to report my story (our story, if you think about it) you will see that what I am doing has an exceptional amount of historical significance, not only locally but universally as well.
  So, who am I?
  I do need a name - a cooler name than the one I was born with (Beckett Glidden, yuck), but I feel that these things need to be organic. The name must find me, instead of the other way around. I doubt Jack the Ripper planted that name on his crime scenes around White Chapel. He got his name because of the way he ripped his victims.
  I ripped my victim, too, but I wouldn't think of adopting the legend's moniker.
  There's your first task, Mr. O'Donnell, give me a good name. Something that will strike even more fear into the people of this town.
  I like that Cassidy's mom called me an "Evil Monster from Hell," but that doesn't quite roll off the tongue.
  Anyway, you're the writer. I'll just keep killing and I'm sure a good name will come to you. I'm sure that if you don't come up with something, your

buddies at the police station will give me a nickname (if they haven't already) or the town will come up with something. You should do it, though, it would make it all the more appropriate. The killer and the reporter, linked until death does one of them part.

Who's going to go first, do you think? I'll bet I know.

Let's get down to the nitty gritty though. What will I give you for all of your good reporting work? Well, how about a real scoop.

I'll walk you through the murder and why I chose the one I did.

It was always going to be Halloween. What better night to start my (death) march into infamy? And believe it or not, it was always going to be her, too.

Oh boy, that will really give the boys in blue a mindfuck. I can't wait to read about the hundreds of high school students being interrogated for their involvement. I will state unequivocally that I am not a high school student, but I doubt that will hold much sway with our Detective Leonard. I get the impression that he will not leave a stone unturned.

It won't matter. You can look under every stone on the planet, you won't find me. I am like bin Laden, but better.

I'm not even hiding.

Why Cassidy? Well, I enclosed a clue (did you love it? did you throw up? I did.), but you guys are going to get that all wrong too, looking for Daddy. I am not the daddy and Daddy is not the killer.

I don't think you believe me though.

I watched her a lot on Halloween. I knew her every move and could even sync up my breath and heartbeat with her. I got real close to her, closer than I've ever been to anyone before. It was awesome and I don't mean that in the valley girl sense of the term. The power I felt that night was awe-some.

She did go to a party - Leonard (yes, I figured you'd be reading this too) there was a party and a lot of kids were being naughty. Cassidy had a few drinks, flirted with some boys, booty danced with others, showed off her ta-tas and started walking home.

I know, I was just as shocked as you were. What was a nice girl like Cassidy doing knocked up and drinking? Well, it turns out, kids these days are complex. Lots of shades of grey. She was a kid who tended to keep her nose clean, but still made a few mistakes.

She probably thought she was going to get an abortion (I don't think she would have), and couldn't see the harm in having a few drinks. It's like doing heroin on your deathbed, I suppose. If you're going to die anyway, why the hell not?

It was while she was walking home, passing the Childs Street Theater, that I got in her way, led her astray and started to slay.

That was the best part.

I'm assuming nobody reading this letter has ever murdered a person (and yes, I assume that there are more people reading this than Ken and Det. Leonard), well, let me tell you, it is quite the odd sensation.

When I made my first stab, it was like getting in a car wreck. You can see it coming, and though it happens really fast, it feels like it is going super slow. I was amazed at how much the body naturally resists being stabbed. At first. After she had bled out a bit, the next dozen or so slashes and stabs went really easily.

I discovered my little bonus, lifted it out and put it on ice, waiting to see who would write about me first and get the prize.

Congratulations.

Now, if I can change my tone and get a little serious - this may get a touch scary - you better do everything I say or I will bring even more hurt to this shitty little burg than anyone could ever dream. I am not kidding when I tell you that I will never be found and that I can kill at will. You may get the full story from me one day, if you last, that is, but for now, just do what I tell you to do.

Here are your tasks

1. Place a murdered animal on your doorstep - this lets me know that you are going to play my game. No animal, I will kill you.

2. Try and find me. I know where you should look and if you don't come looking for me, I will think you are uninterested in this game and I'll kill you.

3. This one is for you and Detective Leonard - find my second murder victim. I assure you, I have captured and killed a second resident of Cabot. He or she is out there somewhere. You have 36 hours to find this corpse and report on it (print and web site, please) or I will burn down a building and kill all those who attempt to escape.

Lastly, I want to be sure that I make the top story in every edition of your paper until I am captured, which isn't likely, or everyone in your town is dead, which is more likely than being caught.

What's all this going to accomplish? I don't know. I'll get famous, I guess, and feel more and more omnipotent with every person I kill. You will be able to write the most interesting and most read stories of your life. Hell, you could even make it a book, if you live that long.

That's enough for now. You have your work cut out for you

See you soon (?)

Beckett Glidden

Jerry had read the letter aloud and he dropped the pages on to the table, stunned. Detective Leonard pulled out his cell phone, punched in some numbers and immediately started barking orders.

"Beckett Glidden! Find Beckett Glidden, right now! I want Kachocki and Betsill to go with me to the high school and start questioning everyone who might know Cassidy Samuels, both personally and in the more biblical sense of the word. I'll be bringing in a letter that I want scanned for fingerprints and a full handwriting analysis. Also, see if there are any missing person reports in town and then send every available unit out on the roads, looking for a second body."

Leonard hung up the phone and grabbed the letter.

"Wait, Chris, what do we do now?" Jerry asked.

"I can't answer that for you, Jerry."

"Will you talk to Ken with me? It seems like this Glidden guy is going to do a lot more damage if Ken stops doing his job," Jerry said, pleading. Leonard didn't know if this was out of Jerry's concern for the citizens of Cabot or the fact that without Ken, he had no hard news writer during the biggest story in Cabot history.

"I can't convince a him to stay around here, especially when his life is almost certainly in danger," Leonard said. "I'm sorry."

He looked at everyone in the room, studied their stunned faces and nodded grimly before exiting the building.

Jerry got up immediately afterwards and went upstairs to Ken's desk.

Ken was throwing all of his files and folders into a large, green trash bag.

"Ken -," Jerry started, but Ken put out his hand, stopping him.

"I don't want to know what it said, Jerry. Please. I'm sure this guy wants me to do all sorts of crazy things and he has probably threatened me if I don't do them. I don't want to know the specifics. I just want to get the hell out of here, get my family and go."

Jerry put his hand on his shoulder.

"I understand, but I think you are making a big mistake. Not only are you passing up a chance to write the best stories of your life, but you could be a hero and help capture this psycho."

"No thanks," Ken said, shrugging off Jerry's hand.

"I'll make sure you and your family are protected 24-7 until this guy is behind bars."

"There was a dead baby in a box, Jerry!" Ken screamed. "I saw the girl's body, she was cut wide open and the baby was taken out - to be sent to me! I am fucking scared to death and I am getting the fuck out of here. I don't care about writing stories or being a hero. I care about living and if I have to do that, selling car insurance in Emmaus, Pennsylvania, then so be it."

The two men stared at each other. Ken's eyes glared with anger and fear, while Jerry's glistened with tearful remorse. He had known Ken for years, had given him his big break by hiring him directly from college, and had been at his wedding and the christening of his two kids. Ken was family, everybody at the Clarion was in at least some way, and Jerry knew that he couldn't really protect any of them. He started to worry about his own family and wrote a mental note to send his wife and daughter on a cruise for the next few weeks.

Jerry embraced Ken, who simply stood there and took it for a few seconds before placing his head on Jerry's shoulder and crying.

"I'm sorry. I just can't. I can't," Ken said, standing up, wiping his eyes and leaving the room.

No one in the news room said much if anything for the rest of the day and no one on the Clarion staff attended Cassidy Samuels' funeral.

Around 4 p.m., Jerry came back down to the editorial room and sat down at Ken's desk. He dialed a number and asked Nancy and Susan to come upstairs for an impromptu meeting. When the ladies had pulled up chairs, Jerry began.

"We are at a crossroads, folks. Cabot is going through a tough time and this tragedy is undoubtedly the biggest stories in our careers."

Jerry knew what he wanted to say next. Since Ken quit that morning, Jerry knew there was only one option to save the paper's bacon, but he also knew that the rest of the staff would think it was a terrible option. If this was going to work, he had to make them think it was their idea.

"We all need to step up and pick up Ken's slack, right?" he asked, noting that only Hillary cautiously nodded her head.

"Hillary, are you interested in trying your hand at -"Jerry said.

"No. I believe I am much better suited for the not a matter of life or death beat," she answered.

"Anyone else?" Jerry offered, knowing that no one would take the bait, especially since it meant having a psycho killer playing games with you.

"So, what do we do? A newspaper needs a news department, doesn't it?" he said, loudly, mainly for effect. "Who should we hire?" he asked, tossing in "or rehire?" softly, under his breath.

"Oh no!" said Susan, in a much nastier tone than one would assume could come from a grandmother.

"What?" asked Sam, oblivious to what was being proposed.

Susan pointed an accusing finger across the room at Jerry.

"He wants to bring back Peter Miller," she said, as if the man's name were poison falling from her lips.

"I know we've had problems with him in the past, but," Jerry said, pleading with his team to consider.

"Yes, we've had problems. He threw up on me, twice, and fired guns out the window at people," Hillary said. Both times Peter threw up on Hillary were what ordinary people would consider typical Tuesday mornings, but for Peter Miller, the phrase, "typical Tuesday morning" was not in his vocabulary. Peter was a heavy drinker and drug addict, a paranoid personality and, mainly, just an asshole.

"He stole my car, procured a prostitute in it, did his business and then promptly got arrested," Susan said. "I had to pay to get it out of the impound lot and Peter threatened to sue me if I garnished his wages to get the money back."

Jerry threw up his hands. They were right, Peter was a train wreck, but he was the only person that Jerry knew that could jump into a situation like this one without having to be babied every step of the way.

"I'm sorry, but I just don't see any other way for us to stay on top of this story. We need a veteran reporter who can step in quickly," Jerry stated. "When this is all over, I promise, I'll kick him to the curb, yet again."

Peter had worked for the Cabot Clarion five different times in the span of 16 years. He had walked out on the paper twice, allegedly moving on to bigger and better things, been fired twice; once for the incident with firing the guns out the window and once for setting fire to the kitchen. He claimed it was an accident, but it was Jerry's experience that Molotov cocktails don't accidentally put themselves together. The last time Peter worked at the Clarion, he just left. He hadn't been fired, though it was certainly looming, and Jerry just let it go thinking that Peter was like an old tomcat, running away to hide and die under someone's porch.

"Has anyone seen him lately?" Jerry asked.

The staff was suspiciously silent.

"I'll call his parents. I'm sure if he is around, he will have asked them for money recently," Jerry said.

"Check the gutters," Nancy said, looking surprised that she had said something so hateful.

"Only if I can't track him down anywhere else," Jerry said, walking back to his office. He turned around before reaching the door.

"Maybe things will be different this time around," he offered. Susan barked out a cackle of laughter.

Chapter 5

Have you ever known a boy, lonely as could be?
A lifetime ago he was a child of the free.
So here he stands alone crying at the sea.
It listens, and moves, and holds him.
Singing, oh.
He don't need us anymore, cause life is just too good.

"Revisited" - OAR (Of a Revolution)

Peter Miller stood outside the White Hen Pantry convenience store, nursing his fourth cup of coffee of the afternoon. He was, as the song says, "waiting for the man" and going back and forth over whether he should be doing this or not.

On the one hand, Peter could really use the "sweet relief" of some premium smoke. After using a week's worth of white crosses, still legal and available at some of the finest convenience stores in America (thank you Mr. Aramathon and your very wise and greedy higher-ups), to work on his 1,267 page science fiction opus, "Planet," he needed to shut his brain off and sleep. On the other hand, smoking marijuana was illegal and buying marijuana was super-illegal. Not only did using break his AA promise, it violated the spirit of the tacit agreement that every member makes as they give themselves up to the "higher power."

Then again, so did abusing barely legal speed. Or did it? Peter debated this question back and forth for a bit.

Peter shifted from foot to foot, wiping his slightly runny nose with the back of his hand. He knew he looked shady and he was sure any minute now a police officer would pull up, ask him what was going on and all hell would break loose. Peter and cops never got along, especially not when Peter was covering the cops and courts beat for the Cabot Clarion. Cops typically do not like the press and that was just fine with Peter. Fuck them. In towns like Cabot, cops weren't good for much but handing out speeding tickets and fucking with guys like Peter, who maybe partied to hard and talked shit a little too loud from time to time. What else is there to do in a rinky-dink town like Cabot? Peter never ran into a problem when he took his show on the road to a city like Boston or Providence. The cops there had to deal with the real bad mothers; the rapists, murderers, gang-bangers and crack smokers. Loudmouth drunks like Peter were practically a part of the scenery.

I should just leave, Peter thought. I'll go rent some pay per porn on cable and whack it until I fall asleep. It may take a movie or two, but it's natural and organic and good for me. I need to do something good for me.

And yet, Peter didn't leave the parking lot. He walked a path in front of the store and then walked out to the pay phone (the last one in America?) and back.

Peter sadly pondered the fact that drug dealers tended to be notoriously unreliable.

Maybe this guy, this kid, was somewhere across the street watching the scene, making sure this wasn't a set up, that Peter wasn't a narc. Peter thought about this and tried to make himself appear as casual as possible, which, for the most over-caffeinated man in the world, was no small feat. He pulled out his cell phone to check the time (what ever happened to watches?) and saw that he missed a call. It was no surprise that he hadn't felt the phone vibrate, considering his body was vibrating with the shifting of the Earth's tectonic plates.

That number looks familiar, thought Peter. Drug dealer familiar, he wondered? No, something older and more ingrained in his psyche. A number he felt he could dial in his sleep, in deep, drunken stupors. Perhaps it was a booty call number? But who's booty would it call? This settled his moral dilemma and would also prevent him from beating his meat to a raw pulp.

He dialed the number and started speaking immediately when he heard it pick up. He wanted to take control of the conversation, especially since he didn't know who the hopefully young lady on the other end would be. He didn't really care and it didn't really matter.

"Hey there, I saw you called," he said, in the sexiest voice he could muster. "That makes me really happy, baby. I've missed you. I was hoping you'd call me and tell me you were needing some loving. I need some too, honey. I still dream about your sweet, moist -"

"Peter!" roared Jerry, interrupting what would surely be the most awkward bit of phone sex he would have ever heard in his life. "This is Jerry Jackson at the Clarion."

Peter was stunned and all he could say was "Jerry."

"I need you to come in here right away," Jerry said, as if it were an order and as if Peter still followed Jerry's orders.

"I'm a little busy right now, Jerry, and I swear I haven't taken anything from your building in over a year."

"Have you read the paper lately?" Jerry asked, wanting to add something mean like, "while you used one for a blanket at night."

"A real paper or your rag," Peter said and Jerry vowed not to pull any more punches with this pompous piece of shit.

"I need to talk with you and because I'm offering you money, I'm sure you'll want to talk with me. Last time I checked, whiskey still costs money," said Jerry.

"I haven't had a drink in over a year, Jerry. Nice talking with you though."

"Wait," Jerry cried out, sorry he had said what he did. He knew that battling alcoholism was no joke. His sister had been fighting the drink, and losing, for as long as he could remember. "I'm sorry. That's great to hear. Really great, actually. Please, Peter, come in here as soon as you can. We need to talk."

"Are you offering me a job?" Peter asked, as a banana yellow Iroc-Z pulled into a handicap space near where he was standing. "Oh shit," Peter said.

"I know you can handle it, Peter. It sounds like maybe you finally got your act together," Jerry said.

"Yo man, sorry I'm late, but I got your treats," said J-Mac, the kid that Peter was scheduled to meet 20 minutes ago.

"What was that?" Jerry asked.

"I'm sorry, son, I think you have me confused with someone else," Peter said. "Run along now."

"Run along?" J-Mac yelped. "You're buying an ounce of hydro from me, holmes."

"Hydro?" Jerry asked aloud. "That doesn't sound clean and sober to me, Peter."

"No, Jerry. I had decided not to buy it," said Peter, trying to get out of this situation without losing a job he hadn't even accepted yet or get shot at by a drug dealer that looked like a fat version of Eminem.

"When did you decide that, motherfucker? You could have called me and told me to stay at home and keep watching re-runs of The Munsters," J-Mac yelled.

Vasha Aramathon opened the door and got into the heated debate.

"Get the fuck off of my property!" he bellowed.

"Shut up, Apu," offered J-Mac, which incensed the storeowner. Aramathon started throwing old, sticky donuts at J-Mac's car.

"I am calling the police. You are parked illegally," he said, throwing three glazed donuts at J-Mac and Peter's heads.

"Peter, what the hell is going on there?" Jerry asked.

"Nothing. I swear. I'm clean. I'm on my way," Peter said.

"He ain't clean, man. This is one filthy son of a bitch, right here. He approached my little sister at the skating rink and asked her if she knew where he could buy some ganja. I actually put on clothes and gassed up my car and now he don't want any..."

Peter laughed, trying to play it off.

"O.K., enough pranking me. I've been officially punked. Good job, Walters. Good to see you, too. Ha-ha. Tell Professor Lawrence I'll see him at the next reunion, you old so and so. Kappa Tau, Kappa Tau, Kappa Tau - and how. I'll be there in five minutes, Jerry."

Peter closed his phone and ran to his car. J-Mac followed for a ways but luckily ran out the energy to keep after him and kick his ass.

The drive from White Hen Pantry to the offices of the Cabot Clarion passed over the Kegler Bridge. Peter always stared over the side as he drove over the bridge, looking at the low-tide (was it always low tide under this bridge?) and remembered wading through there one evening on an acid trip 10-12 years ago. He remembered feeling the muck suck at his shoes as he made giant steps, roaring like Godzilla. He would never be able to forget those zany, drug-addled memories. Perhaps he would finally be "cured" when he no longer wanted to remember them. Peter sadly thought that day may never come.

He pulled into the parking lot of The Clarion, parked his car and entered the place he had called "home" on several occasions in his "adult" life. Peter smiled at the thought that many things in his life had quotation marks around them. He was an "author," "clean and sober," living an "adult" life.

"Hiya, Nancy," he said to the unsmiling face behind the reception desk.

"Hello, Peter," she said, stonily. "Go on upstairs. He's expecting you."

"Thanks," Peter chirped merrily, though he was weighed down with guilt as he made his way upstairs. He had done some really miserable things to the people in this building before and, to be honest with himself (to thine own self be true), it was highly likely that he would do so again. He remembered punching out Nancy's husband, T.J., at the last office Christmas party he attended. If he remembered correctly, T.J.'s main offense was trying to calm Peter down long enough for the staff picture to be taken. The lessons learned that evening, don't drink heavily while on hardcore cold medicine and herbal ecstasy and don't punch guys that outweigh you by 150 pounds.

Peter knocked on Jerry's door.

"Come in," Jerry said and Peter obeyed, already feeling like a dog with his tail between his legs. "Hello, Peter Miller."

"Hey, Jerry."

Jerry studied Peter for a moment before speaking again, as if to answer all of his questions without even speaking. Jerry had to admit that Peter looked better than the last time he had laid eyes on him. When Peter just up and disappeared, he was a gaunt, shaky mess with wild, untamed hair and a shaggy, scraggly beard. Peter looked like one of those militia men that were prominent in some of those northern, midwestern states in the 1990s.

"You're looking, ...better," Jerry said. He couldn't say that Peter looked well. He wasn't as emaciated as he had looked a few years ago, but it wasn't like he looked healthy and robust either. Though in better days he could always be counted on cleaning up well and even be considered handsome, Peter was a week's worth of square meals and sunshine from looking good. He wore a short hair cut and his facial hair was gone, but Peter looked a little sweaty and the rings around his eyes were deep, dark pockets of purple flesh.

"Thanks," Peter muttered, looking past Jerry's head, avoiding eye contact. Old habits die hard, he thought to himself, trying to correct the problem immediately. Peter admitted to himself that he needed this job. He had a very low cash flow, for one thing, and he really needed to get out of his head since that was where he found the most trouble.

"So, I assume you've heard about the murder," Jerry started.

"Yes, the high school girl on the football field" Peter said.

"It's a big story, especially for us, and we need to stay on top of it -"

"And you want Ken and I to work together and beat the big boys," Peter said, trying to stay one step ahead of Jerry. See boss, I'm still quick on my feet.

"Ken is no longer with us," Jerry said, casting his eyes away from Peter.

"What? Why? He's not -" Peter asked, feigning concern. He had worked with Ken briefly during a few of his stints at the paper but the two tended to avoid each other.

Jerry sighed.

"No, he's fine. Peter, we have had contact from the killer," he said, continuing to layout the killer's challenges to Ken and mentioning the fetus in the bottom of the box. Peter, to his credit, didn't flinch and Jerry had to wonder about this guy yet again. He looked at Peter and thought that this guy was such a detached psycho, he probably thought that this was all really cool. Jerry kept a poker face.

"Do I get Ken's salary?" Peter asked.

"Sure." agreed Jerry. Ken's salary was less than what Peter was commanding last time he was on the payroll. "But, Peter, we can't have any shenanigans this time. You've got to stay clean and you've got to be good to us."

Peter nodded. His "sobriety" (there were those pesky quotes again) was really tough. He was a million miles from where we was just six months ago, but it was a daily battle and it wasn't one that he felt strong enough to fight everyday. He had stopped drinking but other smaller addictions of shorter durations took their place. Sometimes it was white crosses or the resin from empty bowls of weed, but other times it was lottery tickets, Hostess cupcakes or pornography.

He was hoping to get hooked on work.

"I can do this, Jerry," Peter said with conviction. "I want to do this. I am a good reporter
and I'm not afraid of this guy. Honestly, I don't really have much to lose."

That was very true. Peter was single. He was estranged from his family and, thanks to being a bastard to everyone, he really had few friends. He could dedicate every waking hour to the story and the case. It was a perfect fit.

"When can you start," Jerry asked.

"Just print me out a new press pass and I'm on it," Peter said. "I have to drop by the police station and get caught up."

"Sounds good," Jerry said, standing up and extending his hand. Peter took it.

"Don't walk out on me," Jerry said, keeping Peter's hand in an intensely firm grip "This will either end with me firing you or you submitting a formal resignation and giving me two weeks notice.'

It could end with me in a body bag, thought Peter, but he just smiled and nodded.

"I'll treat you right, boss."

Jerry walked Peter down the hall to the editorial room.

"Could one of you snap a picture and print Peter here another press pass," Jerry asked the staffers in the room. Hillary glared at the two men from her desk.

Derek volunteered and left the room to grab a digital camera.

Peter practically shivered at the icy reception he was getting, but he wasn't surprised. He knew he deserved everything that was coming his way and, as penance, he stood there silently and tried to absorb it all.

"Shoot any windows out lately," Hillary asked.

"No," he answered quietly. "Not lately."

Hillary harrumphed and turned her attention back to her computer.

"Good to have you back," Jerry said, ready to hightail it back to the warmth of his office.

Derek returned, put Peter about six inches from a light blue wall, and snapped a few shots.

"Your pass will be ready in a few minutes," Derek said, turning from Peter and leaving him standing awkwardly in the middle of the room. He closed his eyes and could practically taste the comforting taste of beer coating his tongue.

Chapter 6

And the streets are full of press men
Bent on getting hung and buried
And the legendary curtains are drawn 'round Baby Bankrupt
Who sucks you while you're sleeping
It's the theater of financiers
Count them, fifty 'round a table
White and dressed to kill

"We are the Dead" - David Bowie

Peter Miller had a long history with the Cabot Police and, unfortunately, not all of it was on a professional basis.

Peter was a lifelong resident of Cabot and he started getting in trouble at the age of 11.

It was a summer day and Peter, who couldn't weasel any money from his parents, a nurse and a cobbler (who cobbles in the second half of the 20th century, seriously?), so he decided to try his hand at swiping some treats from the local Cumberland Farms. Needless to say, he was not a criminal mastermind.

His first mistake was trying to steal ice cream sandwiches. To make sure he could get them out of the store without being seen, Peter wore a long sleeve shirt (not suspicious at all in the middle of July) because wearing long pants would draw attention. He entered the store, waved at the lady behind the counter, Myrtle, a frizzy-haired, chain smoker, who knew all the kids by name. Peter thought this was because Myrtle was friendly, but it was really because she didn't trust any of the little shits in the neighborhood further than she could throw them.

Peter made his way to the ice cream cooler and tucked two ice cream sandwiches up each sleeve. His fingers bent over to hold his cuffs closed and started to walk towards the door. Myrtle stared at him. She expected every kid who ever crossed the threshold into her store to try this at some point and now it was Peter Miller's turn.

"How ya doin' Peetah," Myrtle said with one of the hardest accents in the area.

Peter looked around expecting there to be some other person named Peter in the store. He pointed to himself with one of his awkward claw hands, as if asking, "Who me?" Myrtle nodded.

"Oh, I'm fine," he said, getting nervous and shivering with the cold ice cream numbing the veins around his wrists. Could this possibly kill him, he wondered? He started to think it might.

"Nothing look good today, Peetah?" the increasingly witch-like lady said.

"Hmm? Oh, no. I was looking for -" Peter started, changing his mind. If he continued with this line of conversation about a certain item he was looking for, Myrtle might go back there with him and help him look. "I was just browsing. You know, seeing what was new. Nothing was new. So, I'll check back later."

"Your ahms are dripping, Peetah," Myrtle said with an amused tone but a deadly serious face. Peter glanced at his arms and his mouth dropped wide open. He began to stammer something he felt sounded like an apology.

"Save it champ. I'm cawling the cops," Myrtle said, picking up the phone. Peter began to pee himself and Myrtle quickly ushered him outside the store.

"Don't move or I'll have them chahge you with fleeing the law," Myrtle warned, wagging a smelly, yellow-tipped finger in his face. Officer Billy Woodfin, chief of the Cabot police now, pulled in to the parking lot of the store and stepped out of the police cruiser looking like he was eight feet tall and ready to wrestle a bear with his bare hands. He glanced at the melty, soaking mess that was Peter with nary a smirk on his face and entered the store. Inside, he and Myrtle chuckled at the boy and his predicament. To them, this was a slam dunk. Peter was so embarrassed and filled with dread and guilt, he would've spanked himself silly if he could.

Woodfin exited the store and got down to eye level with Peter, unsnapping the holster holding his gun.

"If you ever steal from anywhere in this town again, you will be going up the river for a mighty long time, you read me?" Woodfin said in a soft, but somehow threatening voice.

Peter nodded, squeezing out a couple more drops of pee in his pants. His hands were now sticky with the almost completely melted ice cream and they were starting to get caked with the chocolate wafers that held the summer treat.

"Go home and tell your parents what you did," Woodfin said. "I'll be calling to make sure you did, Peter, and if you don't tell them you'll be in even more trouble. Now, get out of here."

Peter ran home trying to avoid his legs touching his soaking underwear any more than they had to.

Reflecting on this incident as an adult, Peter smiled at the absurdity of the situation and his naiveté, but still thought Myrtle was an evil bitch. He was glad that he had perfected his skills over the years and had gone back and swiped a box of ice cream sandwiches and six cartons of cigarettes. If cigarettes are like gold in jail (which Peter knew from experience they were, thanks to a violation of parole charge), they were like silver in high school. That one boost, completed thanks to a series of diversions constructed by him and several of his friends, had his little band of thieves treated like kings for a period of close to two months. A period that introduced Peter to things like girl's bare breasts, pornography (only in magazines or on VHS back then), beer and marijuana.

If only he had followed Woodfin's advice, things might have turned out completely different, Peter thought as he pulled in to a space behind the police station. Oh well, you couldn't change the past.

Peter entered the brick building from a door in the back, passing two officers who eyed him suspiciously as he passed by.

"You don't believe in coming to the front desk," Detective Leonard asked.

"Sorry, I've been brought in the back so many times before, I didn't realize there was another entrance," Peter retorted snarkily. He and Chris Leonard had known each other since middle school. They weren't friends, as Peter really didn't have any friends, but they were familiar with each other and Chris knew that Peter, who may be an asshole from time to time, was rarely a malicious asshole.

"So, you're back at The Clarion, I take it?" Leonard asked.

"Call me murder boy," Peter said, quickly adding, "actually, don't."

Leonard smiled, while Peter glanced around the police station. It was the busiest he had ever seen it. There was someone on every phone and officers milled about and marked points on a map of the town.

"Can we talk on the record?" Peter asked.

"Yeah, quickly," Leonard said, leading him to his small, windowless office.

"Nice place," Peter said sarcastically.

"Thanks, it's what seniority gets you." Leonard joked, glad to have his mood lightened a little. He had lived a lifetime worth of long, dark days lately.

"So, Detective Leonard, where are we at right now with the Samuels case?" Peter asked, feeling like Bambi on his new legs as he posed his first news reporter question in years.

Leonard grimaced a little, drew a breath, leaned back and started talking.

"We have no Beckett Glidden in our system, but all that means is that no Beckett Glidden has ever been arrested, in this state or any other," Leonard said, rubbing at his right eye with his right forefinger. It was a tic, but one that Peter didn't think meant that he was lying.

"We also have no missing person reports in town and there are no children in any of the area schools that have any unexcused absences. There are obviously a lot of people in town that live alone and these people may not be noticed as missing for a few more days at least," Leonard, continued, gesturing for Peter to write this next bit down. "We are encouraging people to look in on their neighbors and make sure that all of their friends, family members and acquaintances are accounted for."

Peter scribbled away in his thin, white notebook and buzzed a little at the news juices starting to flow.

"What about the tasks in the letter. Jerry briefly touched on them but he couldn't quote them verbatim. Have you done what he asked?" Peter said, accepting the letter handed to him by Leonard. He scanned the pages, while Leonard spoke.

"We have put a dead animal on Ken's doorstep. It is a black cat and you can thank the Cabot Animal Shelter for donating the corpse," Leonard said. "You don't have to write that, though. Ken and his family have already left town, but we don't know if Beckett Glidden knows that or not."

"Obviously, you have tried to find him, but have you looked where he wants you to look?" Peter asked, knowing it was a stupid question, one of those necessary evils when you're a reporter. It may be dumb, but it's the only way to get the person you're interviewing to talk about that topic.

"We can't know where he thinks we should look, but we have scoured the town and knocked on the door of every Glidden, but those seem too obvious," Leonard said. "If this guy is somewhere in Cabot, he has most certainly seen the Cabot police force at its most mobilized. He knows we are looking for him. My guess is his name isn't really Beckett Glidden and he was watching the houses of all the Gliddens in town."

Leonard rubbed his face at the bridge of his nose. This whole thing was even more frustrating because of this stupid letter. It pointed the police in directions they wouldn't necessarily go to normally. Leonard made this point to Chief Woodfin, arguing that it was likely all a ploy to throw them off track, but Woodfin wouldn't bite. He said they didn't have much else to go on, so they should just stick to the plan of following the letter.

"How many hours do you have left before -" Peter asked.

"You mean, how many hours do we have left," Leonard corrected, pointing from himself to Peter. "If you have replaced Kenny at the Clarion, you have to assume that Glidden wants you to take on his tasks."

Peter had assumed this, but was hoping that it would be a moot point before too long.

"How much time is left?" Peter asked.

"Roughly 24 hours before all hell breaks loose. And remember, you'll have to have a story in tomorrow's paper and he wants a 'cool name.' No pressure or anything," Leonard said.

"Right. No problem," Peter said.

The two men sat staring towards each other for a few moments, but their focus was on other things, mainly this giant sword hanging over their heads.

"You want to go for a ride?" Leonard asked. Peter nodded and they exited the building and got in Leonard's Ford Explorer.

The two rode silently through the streets of Cabot. They passed the library, its windows glowing warmly and the front steps bathed in a simulated moonlight from two floodlights on the lawn. Leonard took a right and drove towards the beach. Peter could just make out the foam of the whitecaps cresting and pounding towards the shore. As they passed an ancient cemetery on the left, Leonard's radio, which had squawked with nonsensical static interrupted by brief moments of human voices, lit up with activity and people speaking loud and clear.

"All units, report to Berrywood Park, Code 2," the dispatcher spoke and Leonard started to accelerate the vehicle.

"What's a Code 2?" Peter asked nervously anticipating the rolling over of the SUV as Leonard weaved around corners of the deserted streets.

"It just means no lights or sirens," Leonard said. "Sometimes we use it so that a perpetrator is unaware we're coming, but tonight I have a feeling its because we don't want any gawkers."

Berrywood Park was the town's crown jewel. It was a peninsula of green space filled with picnic areas, a playground, an amphitheater and beaches on either side. Perhaps the most unique aspect of the park was the Enchanted Garden. Built in the early 20th century by an enterprising pair of young women, the garden was made to look like something from the pages of the books they had been reading since they were children. It was created to look like a place where fairies and elves would make their homes, but it also had elements that made one think of princesses and knights and of clandestine, romantic moonlit walks. The garden was where every high school senior would come to have their prom pictures taken. More than a few people had received their first kiss or more somewhere in that garden, Peter included.

Peter had a bad feeling that whatever they were going to find at the park would be in the Enchanted Garden and it would not be good.

Leonard's SUV slowed as it made its way down the giant hill to the parking lot of Berrywood Park. A uniformed officer with a baby face had unlocked a chain and waved Leonard through, saluting as the vehicle passed. Leonard drove several hundred yards down the road and saw two parked police cars aiming their headlights and a supplemental light through the entrance of the garden.

Peter thought of the creepy inscription on the brick entrance that he read every time he entered the garden.

> *"Whosoever enters here,*
> *let him Beware*
> *for he shall Nevermore*
> *escape nor be free of my spell"*

Not exactly the type of thing you wanted to hear when you were going to head off to prom or attend someone's wedding, but to each his own.

Detective Leonard and Peter exited the SUV and started to walk towards the entrance. The temperature had dropped considerably since Peter had been waiting to score drugs in the parking lot of the convenience store and he was sorely under dressed for the occasion.

"Reiser, you have a parka in your trunk?" Leonard asked in the direction of one visibly shaken officer standing guard at the opening of the garden. Reiser nodded and Leonard reached in to the driver's side of the car and popped the trunk. He tossed the parka at Peter.

"I think we're going to be out here awhile," he said.

Peter put the parka on and he and Leonard entered the garden and approached a small gathering around the fountain, which had been shut down for the season. Peter was trying to see what was drawing the crowd's attention, while also knowing that once he saw the treachery that lay before him, he would never be able to unsee it. He had seen a lot of terrible shit in his day, but so far he had been able avoid seeing a mutilated body.

That train left the building seconds later as the officers parted ways to allow the detective and Peter in to the cluster to see the body.

It was beyond horrible.

Once again, the victim was a female, but this one looked much older than 17. She was completely naked, which seemed very wrong on a night where temperatures were quickly dropping into the teens. Peter gagged a little as he took note of all the open wounds on the body. The killer, Glidden most likely, had opened the woman's flesh in long strips down each of her limbs, making each limb look like that of a dissected frog. Her blood made a large but shallow pool around her. It looked thick and Peter wondered at what temperature blood started to freeze.

"How long has she been out here," Leonard wondered aloud.

"The blood isn't hot and it is starting to freeze," a female officer named Tweedy said, holding out a gloved finger to show that she touched the puddle while still following all appropriate police procedures.

"So, that means what, hours?" Leonard asked angrily.

"This has been one of our regular stops since the murder and all was normal at the last check in around 3 p.m.," Tweedy said.

If Glidden had been here, it was likely somewhere between 4:30 and 5:30 p.m. There had been some daylight around then, but the park tended to be fairly empty in the off-season.

Peter absorbed all of the police-speak, but his gaze kept going back to the dead woman. She hadn't been cut open at the gut like Cassidy had, but there had to be some meaning behind this woman's skin being peeled open to reveal the insides of her limbs. Peter also noted the look of fear on her face. Obviously she was scared at being killed, but he imagined that the cutting had been done while she was still alive and she had died soon after, before her face could go slack while she bled out.

"Any ideas on who she is?" Leonard asked no one in particular. Everyone present shook their heads.

Peter took a step back and started to look around the area to see if Glidden had left any clues, written or otherwise, but he couldn't see anything.

"We've fingerprinted her and sent it over to be run through the system, but nothing yet," Tweedy said.

"And no clues, nothing written anywhere?" Leonard asked.

"Haven't seen anything, but we have stayed close to the body since we got here," reported Tweedy.

Leonard nodded.

"Bag up the body and take it to the morgue. No need to examine it in the freezing cold," Leonard ordered. "I also want everyone to comb the park for clues immediately. Peter, follow me."

Peter did as he was told, following Leonard as they headed towards the left wall and started to walk the brick path. Leonard swept his flashlight from left to right with his gun ready to start blasting away if he saw anybody nefarious during their search. They didn't see anything, but at the top of the garden, where a small sheltered balcony overlooked the garden, Peter noticed that some of the bricks by the entrance looked discolored and out of place. He pointed it out to Leonard and they jogged over to the area, the cold air starting to burn Peter's lungs and making him want to spit. He held it in though, not knowing the etiquette of a crime scene.

They quickly saw what was wrong with the bricks. The pieces of the woman's skin that had been cut were taped to the wall with duct tape and on her skin was a message.

"Perhaps this is the cruelest cut of all
the cut that one can feel and see.
Is it wrong to want someone
to share this experience with me?"

Leonard motioned for the crime scene photographer to come over and take pictures. After the photos were taken, Leonard peeled off the tape and placed the strips of flesh in plastic evidence bags. He handed the bags over to an officer who was standing by the crew moving the woman's body into a body bag and on to a gurney. The phrase, " a pound of flesh" flashed in Peter's mind.

"Come on, Peter. Let's go," Leonard said, already walking away towards his SUV.

Peter walked on unsteady legs and took deep breaths to try and slow his rapidly beating heart and hold back wave after wave of nausea.

"We'll talk back at the station about what you should write," Leonard said, again sounding very officious. Peter decided he wouldn't question the order and thought that if this were a year ago, this would be the start of an ugly scene that would result in Peter getting either beat up or arrested.

Leonard took the long way back to the police station, winding his way past Elkington Pond and over the hill that led down towards the hospital. They passed their old middle school and the ball field where both had played baseball. Peter believed that Leonard was using this time to process what he had seen, but really Leonard was trying to get control of his emotions. If he didn't settle down, he was likely to start whaling on the first person that gave him static and, knowing his old middle school chum the way he did, it was very likely to be Peter. He was glad the reporter gazed out at the sights and remained quiet.

Eventually, Leonard calmed down enough to go back to his office and Peter obediently followed. He hadn't had to make any real decisions since taking his old job back, but he would be on his own very soon. It would be him and his computer screen and the words he chose would have serious ramifications. He was glad to have someone to bounce ideas around with, but he knew that he would write what he felt he had to write and the police would either accept it or they wouldn't.

"Let me see if the Chief is here," Leonard said, rising from his seat almost as soon as he had sat down.

Peter gazed around Leonard's office and started to take in the details or lack thereof. There were no pictures of a wife or family and, outside of a few certificates, the only things that hung on the wall were a few illustrated safety posters that tend to be hung up in schools. Peter understood that Chris Leonard lived as spartan a life as he did and that his addiction was police work.

Chief Billy Woodfin entered the office and Peter stood up and offered his hand. Woodfin smiled but didn't take it.

"You're still around here, huh? I thought I had run you out of town outside of that store when you were 11," Woodfin said and Peter forced a small smile.

"Alright fellas, we got number two, but we still don't know who she is, huh?" Woodfin asked. Leonard shook his head and Woodfin pointed at Peter. "Get Tommy Gates to draw you a picture of our victim - ask your readers if they can help identify her," Woodfin said and Peter rankled a bit at taking orders from the Chief.

"Next, this psycho wrote another message, are you going to include it in your article?" Woodfin asked and Peter had to pause. He had gotten so used to being told what he was going to do that he hadn't really thought about it.

"I'd like to -" Peter started to say, but Woodfin jumped right in again.

"Good. You should. He wants to get his stuff in the paper and we should play along right now. Maybe it jogs somebody's memory out there and points us in the right direction," Woodfin said.

"What about running his letter?" Peter asked.

"That's up to your boss," Woodfin said. "I could argue both for it and against it."

"This guy said he wants a name, Chief, what should Peter call him" Leonard asked.

"I was thinking 'The Cabot Butcher'," Peter offered and Woodfin nodded.

"Yeah, that's good. It may even offend him if he thinks he is doing more than just cutting up meat," Woodfin said. "'The killer, who police are referring to as 'The Cabot Butcher', struck again last night.' There's your first sentence." Woodfin said. Peter had to admit it was good and he was likely to use it, but he was starting to feel a little offended. Peter wouldn't think of telling the cops how to do their jobs. At least not now. When he was sobering up in the drunk tanks, he felt compelled to offer his advice, but there was no stupid juice in his system now.

Leonard started to pace around the office a little bit.

"We need to try and lay a trap somewhere in the story," Leonard said. "Something that may throw this guy off his game enough to make a mistake."

"What did you have in mind?" Woodfin asked.

"I don't know," Leonard said. "Maybe we put something in there like there police are narrowing in on a suspect and an arrest is expected to happen soon. Then we stage a fake arrest scene and see if our guy is in the area peeking in."

"It couldn't hurt," Woodfin admitted. "We'll use your web site too, so that you can put something like arrest imminent and then leave your office to go cover it," he said to Peter, whose eyes widened as he realized he would be the bait.

"You're going to use me as bait?" he asked incredulously.

Woodfin stood up angrily, his face taut and burning red, and pointed a finger in Peter's face.

"All the fucked up shit you did in this town and you're going to balk at helping stop a serial killer? I don't think so! You do what you're fucking told or I'll throw you in a cell so fast your head will spin!" Woodfin said. Peter's face flushed. His relationship with cops would never change, but he wasn't going to challenge him. He would help them and when this was all over he was going to get the hell out of this rusty bear trap of a town once and for all.

Chapter 7

Confusion Prince is at my door
The crown I wear is the one he wore
He's here to bring me down some more and bend my mind
The friendly stranger calls my name
He only wants me for his game
But it don't matter just the same I bend his mind

"Confusion Prince" - Grateful Dead

'Butcher' strikes again
By Peter Miller
pmiller@theclarion.com

The killer, who police are referring to as 'The Cabot Butcher', struck again last night.

The victim, yet to be identified (see photo), was found at the center of the Enchanted Garden at Berrywood Park early yesterday evening. The scene was once again very gruesome and officers and EMTs on the scene were sickened by the amount of carnage inflicted by the killer.

"It is hard to believe that someone can be this sick and depraved," said Detective Chris Leonard. "Whoever is committing these atrocious acts is more animal than human. The killer should know that animals can be hunted and captured."

Police believe that this murder was committed by the same person who murdered former Cabot High School junior Cassidy Samuels and Leonard and Cabot Police Chief Billy Woodfin believe they are close to closing in on arresting a suspect.

"This person has told us his name. He wants to be caught and we are going to be happy to oblige," Woodfin said. "I expect an arrest will be made soon."

The Clarion received a letter from the killer after the first articles about the Samuels murder hit the streets. The letter was addressed to former writer Ken O'Donnell, who has since taken a leave of absence from the publication, and featured a number of challenges to both O'Donnell and members of the Cabot Police Department.

Here is an excerpt from the letter:

"I want to be sure that I make the top story in every edition of your paper until I am captured, which isn't likely, or everyone in your town is dead, which is more likely than being caught.

What's all this going to accomplish? I don't know. I'll get famous, I guess, and feel more and more omnipotent with every person I kill. You will be able to write the most interesting and most read stories of your life. Hell, you could even make it a book, if you live that long.

That's enough for now. You have your work cut out for you.

See you soon (?)"

"The Cabot Butcher" has taken over the pages of the newspaper and dominates the evening news, but police believe these are all the machinations of an ego-maniacal psychopath who craves attention. Cabot Clarion publisher Jerry Jackson has stated that this will be the only excerpt of the killer's letter that will ever be published in his publication.

"We don't negotiate with maniacs," said Jackson. "We printed this as a favor to our local law enforcement, but we will not kowtow to any more demands."

Police are asking that if you can identify the woman in the picture on the front page or have any information on The Cabot Butcher to please contact them immediately. The town's curfew for teens is still in effect and police are encouraging all Cabot residents to follow the curfew and report any suspicious activity.

The police station started to get flooded with calls, but none led them any closer to identifying the second victim or an actual arrest. Other than two officers who drove towards the center of town from opposite directions, really just to give the impression that all was well and everyone was safe, the rest of the police force manned the phones to write down all the messages coming in.

Many of the calls felt that the woman in the picture looked like either a distant relative of theirs or a younger version of actress Susan Sarandon. Leonard had to agree, she did kind of look like a "Rocky Horror Picture Show" era Susan Sarandon. He shook his head though when he thought about the possibility of nobody identifying her and having to give her a pauper burial behind St. John's Cathedral.

As for clues to the identity of the killer, there were a few people calling in to claim they were him, but none of them knew the name that the killer signed his letter with. Leonard wondered what would drive people to do something like claiming they were a murderous maniac and he couldn't come up with anything.

Sometimes it felt like the whole world was going crazy.

Later that afternoon, after hundreds of calls, Woodfin called Leonard into his office.

"I think it's time we bait the trap," he told his detective.

Leonard nodded. He agreed that they had very little to go on and he felt that this killer was being very observant, viewing the proceedings like a chess game. He just hoped that the psycho wasn't expecting the police to try to bluff him into a trap. If he expected it, Peter Miller could wind up dead, and asshole or not, he didn't deserve to be savagely murdered.

"I'll call Peter," Leonard offered.

"Tell him to post the story around 10 a.m. tomorrow and then to leave his office immediately, speeding all the way to us. If he's being trailed, we'll want to see the person following him trying to keep up," Woodfin said.

The plan was for Peter to race across town to a home the police had set up for drug and prostitution stings. It was a pretty good plan, assuming that 'The Butcher' was always watching, as he claimed he was, but things could go wrong. Leonard vowed that he wasn't going to let Peter die on his watch. Peter had gone along with this scheme and was really trying to be a team player. Leonard, who had dealt with his share of drunks, both recovering and backsliding, figured that Peter must have had a moment of clarity awhile back and was now trying to right past wrongs. There were a lot of wrongs in his past too, so Leonard wanted to make sure Peter had a time to right them all.

Leonard dialed the number of the Cabot Clarion and asked for Peter.

"Is he in trouble again?" Nancy asked. "That certainly didn't take long."

"No, he isn't in trouble," Leonard chuckled. "Is he in?"

"Yes. Hold please."

She forwarded the call to Peter's desk and he picked up immediately.

"Peter Miller," he answered.

"Peter, it's Chris. We want you to put the story on the web site around 10 a.m. tomorrow, O.K.?"

Peter didn't respond for a minute, but finally croaked out a "yes."

"Are you nervous?" Leonard asked.

"Yes, of course I am," Peter snapped, answering in a hushed tone. "If this works the way you think it will, I'm going to have a fucking killer chasing me to a fake arrest scene."

"Relax, Peter. Nothing will happen to you. We're going to post an officer in your neighborhood tonight and another officer will be tailing you when you leave your office tomorrow. If anybody else is following you, we'll know right away and we'll catch this son of a bitch," Leonard explained.

"Yeah, but -" Peter couldn't finish. There were a million buts, the main one being, but what if he doesn't follow me. What if he lets us play out this bluff, makes us look stupid and then kills me later that night for daring to mess with him.

"Look, Peter. I'm proud of you. You stepped right in to this situation and are obviously trying to make amends for some of your past actions. That's commendable. So, don't stop now," Leonard said.

"Yuh," Peter grunted. "I'll see you tomorrow." He hung up the phone and chewed on what Leonard had just said. He was trying to right past wrongs, even if he didn't realize it. He was back at the paper where he had caused the most trouble and hurt the most people and was now doing a job that nobody else could do or even wanted to do. He was helping the police, and not because he had been caught doing something illegal and was avoiding jail by doing it, which is the way he always thought it would go down. He was helping them save his town from a savage beast and as much as he hated the town because of all the painful memories that were made there, he did not want to see it destroyed. He started to smile and nod at his realizations.

"Are you all high right now?" Hillary asked.

Not everybody could see what Peter was doing, of course, but that was alright. He wasn't doing it for the glory. Leonard had said something about making amends and Peter recalled that making amends was one of the steps he had heard about in one of the few meetings he had attended.

"No," he said.

"Uh-huh," she said dubiously.

"Hillary, I, uh, let me just apologize for everything I've done in the past, O.K.?," he started. Hillary nodded and put up a hand to stop him. She picked up a nearby phone and hit the intercom button.

"Everybody, please report to the editorial room, Peter is going to apologize," she announced, placing the phone back in its cradle.

"What the hell?" Peter asked.

"Look, Peter. If you're sincere about apologizing, you have a lot of apologies to make to everyone here, you might as well get them all out of the way at once," Hillary said.

He glared at her, not wanting to apologize to her at all anymore. Susan and Nancy entered together from downstairs, while Derek came in a few moments after they did. He had stopped in the kitchen to re-fill his coffee cup. Jerry came in after Derek and Sam turned in his seat to face Peter.

"Go ahead," Hillary said, moving back to her seat. Peter blushed and cleared his throat.

"Umm, I was hoping to make this more personal and private and, you know, take my time and wait until it was appropriate," Peter said.

"No time like the present," interrupted Susan.

"Right.," Peter agreed. "Well, let me just start by thanking Jerry for the opportunity to come back. If any of you had anything to do with that decision -"

"We didn't," Hillary said. Peter looked at her, noting the angry glare in her eyes. He knew he had probably hurt her the most. They had, very briefly, been a bit of an item and, even during some of his really low times, she had defended him longer than anyone else.

"O.K., well, I'm glad to be back and I hope that we can become a great team. I am really sorry about everything I did in the past," Peter said.

"Like what?" Derek asked.

"Like everything, Derek. O.K.? Fine, you want me to list it all off, I will. I'm sorry for shooting my gun out the windows, I'm sorry for puking on you Hillary and I'm sorry for punching everyone I ever punched. I'm sorry for stealing sodas, forgotten lunches, money from the snack jar and the delivery van. I'm sorry for having sex with that skanky cheerleader on the conference room table and on the sink in the woman's room and against the paste-up bank."

"The what?" Sam asked.

"Before we could lay out everything on the computer, we pasted it up - never mind, but sorry I soiled it," Peter said. "I'm sorry I soiled everything. I was, Hell, I guess I still am a bit of a fuck-up, so I'm sorry. I've had a lot of problems and I never dealt with them well, I just replaced one problem with another. I don't drink anymore and I don't get high anymore, all that much, if ever, and never on work time."

He looked around the room as he tried to catch his breath and think about what he should say next.

"None of you have to like me and I don't blame you if you don't or can't," Peter said, adding, "But I am trying and I just want you to know that I now want to be forgiven and for me, that's a huge step. That's it. Again, I'm really, really sorry, for everything."

He sat down at his desk, cast his eyes down and started typing his bait story that he would post in the morning. His colleagues looked at each other, impressed by the amount of honesty that their former degenerate co-worker had spoken with. Jerry was perhaps the most impressed and a smile crept over his face as he turned around and walked back to his office. Derek, Nancy and Susan quietly spoke with each other as they made their way back downstairs. Hillary approached Peter's desk.

"Apology accepted," she said, turning around quickly and going back to her desk.

Nobody spoke again in the office for the remaining few minutes of the work day.

After writing the story, Peter shut down his computer and left for the day. He drove around looking for a fast food place to pull into and started to think about tomorrow's action-packed morning. He was definitely nervous and mainly because he had rarely put himself in situations like this, even in his drug-crazed, guns blazing days. The closest thing to this was when he "drove get-away" during a drug heist. He never had to really drive all that crazy and the incident went off without a hitch, but the anticipation that he felt while sitting in the car, waiting for his friends to come running out of the house, burned and boiled in his guts.

He drove them to the parking lot of a run-down shopping plaza with a donut shop and a third-rate Chinese restaurant serving as anchors.

"This guy's house is a couple of blocks over and he has ounces and ounces of weed stashed in a vacuum sealed container in his basement," his friend, Jeremy, said regaling him and their friend Mickey with the tale, as if it were a trunk of buried treasure. Jeremy had discovered it while helping a buddy of his with a small construction job at the house a few weeks before. "We know this guy is out of town today, so Mickey and me are going to sneak into the basement, grab the stuff and get out of there. It's fool-proof, because, the guy will eventually notice the stuff is missing, but doesn't he know us from a hole in the ground and what's he going to do, call the cops and say his weed was stolen?"

Jeremy made a convincing argument.

"You just wait here, Pete. Keep the keys in the ignition and get ready to drive when we get back," Jeremy said, as he and Mickey exited the car and started to walk towards the drug house.

Peter nodded and sat in the car, facing forward towards the counter to the right of the cash registers of the donut shop. He studied the stooped frames and flabby backsides of the people who were enjoying their coffee and donuts at 2 p.m. in the afternoon. As someone aiding and abetting a breaking and entering he hated to judge people, but what were these people doing eating donuts so late in that afternoon. What exactly were they taking a break from?

Time felt like it wasn't passing very quickly, but Peter noted that his friends had been gone for over 10 minutes. He must have looked really fishy just sitting in a parked car in a parking lot. He tried to concoct a reasonable excuse, in case anyone asked him what he was doing, and settled on waiting on his friend while he got a haircut at the salon. This wouldn't hold up, of course, but it might buy him some time to craft a second excuse top place on top of the first one.

Once the 15 minute mark had passed, Peter started to panic. They had obviously been caught, thought Peter, either by the police or by the guy who was supposed to be gone, and their captors would be coming to the car very soon. Peter wiped at his sweaty brow and tried to think about what his course of action should be. He thought of the famous song by The Clash and started to hum, "Should I stay or should I go?"

If he stayed, very soon uniformed police officers would be knocking on his window, asking him to please step outside. Or worse, drug-crazed gang members would be chasing after Jeremy and Mickey and they would be stopped trying to get in the car and all three of them would then be dragged out and beaten to a pulp.

Peter had spent three minutes daydreaming about both of those horrible scenarios and his friends had yet to return.

I'll leave, he thought, they can borrow my car, if they come back, and I'll just walk home. He stepped out of the car, double and triple checking that he was leaving the car unlocked with the keys in the ignition.

Of course, this looked really sketchy too, assuming that people had been watching him in the first place. Aside from how suspicious it made him look, he could also have his car stolen by one of these shady, 2 p.m. donut eaters, who were obviously just waiting for the right time to burst into action.

He got back in the car, pounded on the steering wheel and screamed "Fuck" at the top of his lungs. One of the donut eaters turned around on his swivel stool. Apparently, he had great hearing and Peter's car was not sound-proofed.

Now if he got out of his car, the donut-eater might think he was challenging him.

He decided to collect the trash in his car, toss it all in a loose fast food bag and then throw it away in the barrel outside of the donut shop. Less than five seconds after Peter had stooped down to start collecting loose straw wrappers and empty cigarette boxes, Jeremy and Mickey jumped in the car.

"Go!" Jeremy shouted at the same time Peter screamed in fear.

Peter's adrenaline was racing as he backed up the car, narrowly missing an accident with an elderly woman in a walker on her way to the Chinese restaurant.

His friends had successfully robbed the drug dealer and the group was never caught. They smoked free weed for the rest of the year. The lesson Peter learned that day, was not crime will damage your heart, mind and soul, but rather, sometimes crime does pay.

Lucky for Peter, there wasn't much waiting to be done once he posted the story to the web site the next morning. Sure, the night before had been sleepless and Peter looked like a complete wreck in the few hours that he spent in the office that morning, but once the story was up, Peter was a man on a mission.

"I'll be back later, Nancy. Looks like the cops might finally have their man," he shouted back to the receptionist as he exited the building.

Both Woodfin and Leonard did not want Peter to tell anyone that he worked with that this was a set-up. Jerry wouldn't like it in the first place. Not only did it put one of his reporters in mortal danger, but it was placing an entirely inaccurate story on his web site.

Peter got in his car and backed out of his space rapidly. He kept glancing in his rear-view mirror and saw nobody. He could not decide whether this was a good thing or a bad thing.

Peter raced over the bridge and squealed his tires as he maneuvered the car around a tight right turn at the train tracks. He hung an immediate left and passed through one of Cabot's few truly scary neighborhoods. Known to many as the Iron Triangle, Peter had spent his share of time in some of the musty, poorly constructed apartment buildings there, but today, like many days in the past few years, he just sped on through. Even though all the familiar tastes started to dwell on his tongue every time he passed by. Just seeing the abandoned, rusty cars on the sidewalk and the stained beige buildings with broken windows on the front doors made him think of smoking cigarettes, getting drunk on Grape Kool-Aid and vodka and taking heavy, lung clogging bong hits.

After finally reaching the end of the road through the Iron Triangle, Peter passed several used car lots and a lumber yard where his cousin used to work.

He glanced in the mirror once again and still saw nothing. Peter increased his speed, turned a hard right and got a little bit of air as his car passed over another set of train tracks. He was in the home stretch, speeding down a four lane road past a small brick deli and heading towards a playground. After he passed the playground, he could see the final turn he had to make. A large church where he had taken piano lessons for a few years back in elementary school stood across the street. Peter decided to slow just a little bit instead of stopping, just to make sure the coast was clear, before banging that final left and reaching the house. As he nosed to the intersection and glanced left, his car was rocked by a collision that smashed the driver's side door and flipped the already off-kilter vehicle over. Peter was dazed and obviously in a great amount of pain and in a state of shock. He did smile though because there would be a police officer coming up behind him any minute.

Chapter 8

I've just seen a face
I can't forget the time or place where we just met
She's just the girl for me
I want all the world to see we've met

"I've Just Seen A Face" - The Beatles

Peter's eyes fluttered, before opening in a panic. His car had just been struck, it was being pushed over and he couldn't remember what had happened next. He had to get out before it caught fire, before –

"Hey there, sleepy head, you're awake," a woman's voice called out. He tried to turn his head to see her, but it wouldn't move.

"You're O.K., Peter, you are just heavily sedated. You were in a terrible car accident, but you were very lucky. You're alive and, aside from some bumps and bruises, you're perfectly healthy."

Peter exhaled a sigh of relief and, because of the drugs, felt like he could see smoke clouds of his sigh radiating out towards the ceiling.

"Where were you off to in such a hurry?" she asked.

He did not know how to answer this.

"Oh, I see, now that you're awake you're going to be shy with me," the flirtatious woman's voice said. "That's O.K., I understand. I'll be back in a few minutes."

I am in the hospital, Peter thought. I must be. That's where people who have been in serious car crashes go.

Peter wondered how long ago the crash had been and how long he had been out or under sedation. He tried to lift his watch but his arm felt like it weighed a hundred pounds. Everything on his body felt heavy. He was able to lift his head for a split second before it crashed back on to the soft pillow below him.

Perhaps he could turn his head and examine the room. He was able to roll his head a fraction to the right and he directed his eyes in that direction and saw a blur that must be a bedside table. There was a small dresser and a door that he expected led to a bathroom. Over to the left was a door that led out of the room and presumably into the hallways of the hospital, but Peter was starting to doubt that this was a hospital. He had spent a fair amount of time in emergency rooms and had been checked in, sometimes involuntarily, into psychiatric wards to dry out and detox, and this room was way too quiet compared with his time in those rooms.

Peter kept his eye on the door, waiting for the woman to return to his room. He did not have to wait long.

The door swung open seconds after Peter had focused his attention on it and a beautiful woman with long, auburn hair entered carrying a tray with a steaming bowl of soup, a bottle of water and a box of Cheez-Its. Peter was so taken by her beauty, he did not notice if there was a hospital in the hallway behind her.

"Soup's on," she said. "I brought you some Cheez-Its, too, because, well, I like to put them in my soup when I'm having a bad day. And you are having a bit of a bad day, if I do say so myself."

Peter smiled.

"I guess you think so, too, Peter."

"How long have I been here?" Peter asked in a croak. He coughed a bit afterwards in an attempt to clear his throat. The woman opened the bottle of water, placed a straw inside and offered it to him. He immediately started drinking.

"Only two days," she said.

Two days, Peter thought in a panic. He started to examine this woman more closely. She was not wearing scrubs or a doctor's coat.

"Where am I?" Peter asked.

"You're at my home, Peter. I came across your accident the other day. I saw the whole thing. You sped into an intersection and a car rammed you. Your car flipped over several times. I stopped my car to see if you were O.K. and the car that hit you, sped away."

"So, why am I here? Why didn't you call for help?" Peter asked in a high pitched tone.

"I thought I could help you," she said softly. "I did help you," she added, with a tinge of anger in her tone.

"The police would have been there any second," Peter said. "I was on my way to meet them. There was an officer a few blocks behind me, trailing me."

The woman scooted up on the bed and placed her hand on his forehead. It felt soft and warm. God, it had been so long since Peter had been touched by a woman. He felt like weeping.

"He wasn't coming, Peter. I slit his throat about five minutes before you left your office."

Peter screamed and tried to vault himself up and out of the bed, but it was useless. He wasn't going anywhere, she had obviously made sure of that with whatever drug she had given him.

"Just relax," she cooed, stroking his sweaty forehead. "If I wanted you dead, too, I would have run over your head with my car."

Peter struggled for a few seconds more but his muscles burned and he was so tired.

"Allow me to introduce myself. I am Beckett Glidden and you are in the year 2035," she said, getting up from the bed and pulling the curtains open. Despite the fact that Peter thought that this woman was clearly insane, he was expecting to see cars fly by the window. "I know, it's not all that dramatic, but things don't change all that much in a quarter of a century."

"You are a fucking nut, lady!" Peter spat out, once again trying to move. Beckett punched him in the face and his head swam with pain.

"You are being really impolite, my little friend, which is not only very rude, but also very stupid. Need I remind you, I have killed people and not just killed them, but really fucked them up," she yelled. "Push my buttons anymore and I will do my absolute worst on you."

She paced back and forth at the foot of Peter's bed a few times before gazing out the window. Peter tried to catch his breath and swallow the rising panic in his throat.

"I'm sorry, Peter. I brought you here so that I could tell you my story, show you my power and share this world with you -" she said, as if offering a trip on a magic carpet ride.

"You don't even know me," he yelled at her.

"On the contrary, Peter. I've gone back and watched hundreds of moments in your lifetime. I know you as well as you know yourself. You need to know me, Peter."

"If you are the person who killed Cassidy Samuels and that woman we found in the garden the other night, then I know all I need to know," he said.

Beckett nodded and walked to a corner of the room. She turned back around, carrying a roll of duct tape. Beckett ripped off a piece and placed it over Peter's mouth.

"Now, just lie back and listen," she said, starting her life story.

My name is Beckett Glidden. I was born in November of 2007, one month after the Boston Red Sox had won their second World Series of the century. There have been five more since then, by the way. I assume you're a Sox fan, so, you know, it's just good to know that there hasn't been a new curse or anything.

Anyway, my folks were expecting a boy, obviously, and my father was very disappointed when he didn't see a penis. My mom told him we could keep the name Beckett, which was of course in honor of Josh Beckett, the winningest pitcher in Red Sox history. They called me Becky, but my birth certificate reads, Beckett.

My life was fairly normal for a Massachusetts girl. I swam in the ocean in the summer time and went skiing in the winter. I was raised Catholic, of course, but none of that guilt they try to heap on everyone ever really stuck on me. I know there isn't a God and I'm even more sure of that now. I am the most powerful being in the universe, but I'll get to that in a minute.

Anyhoo, there weren't too many unhappy memories growing up. I had a couple pets die, only two at my hand – a hamster and a stray dog that I experimented on towards the end of high school. I wanted to be a veterinarian for the longest time, but life happened – you know, what I mean?

I went to Pioneer Valley Tech, out by Zoo Mass, Mount Holyoke and Amherst, and fell in love. His name was Eric Tremont and he was everything I was looking for at the time, which means he was Mr. Wrong. Eric was a bad boy. He introduced me to all sorts of bad things, things I know you are quite familiar with, Peter, but he also dabbled in drug creation. Despite being a degenerate junkie, Eric was also a brilliant mind. He was an artist with chemicals and he was something of a savant when it came to making special concoctions. He was searching for a legal, less messy form of methamphetamine, and though he didn't find it, he did find something that worked out even better.

Allow me to get a little technical, and that's about the best I can do with this, because my specialty was animals, not chemistry or human biology. The average human only uses something like four percent of their brain. Its pretty pathetic when you think about it, especially when most of the human race would rather sit on a sofa, watch TV and get fat. Eric was looking for a way to stimulate the part of the brain that responds to meth, without all the nasty meth chemicals and its terrible side effects. He never really got there, but he did stimulate a part of the brain that opened up a whole other world of possibilities.

For Eric, it was telekinesis. He started off by moving pencils on a table, graduated to moving his dirty dishes from the living room to the kitchen sink within a week and was lifting cars by the end of the month. He got powerful really fast and then he got really greedy. He wanted me to join him and he shot me up with the same concoction. It didn't do the same thing though. My power was, say it with me now, time travel. It's kind of like that guy's power on that old show "Heroes," except I don't have to go all squinty and I had much better control over how far I went back a lot easier than that cute little Asian guy did.

After the shot, Eric sat me down and told me to focus on moving the pencil across the table. I tried really hard, but it wasn't working. We sat there for over an hour and Eric tried to get me to move all sorts of things. He thought maybe I had pyrokinesis and tried to get me to boil water in a pitcher. He had me try to guess which cards he was holding up behind his back, thinking maybe I had ESP.

"Maybe I'm just not cut out for this experiment, babe. Or maybe you're just special," I said.

He got super pissed, as he often did after staying up for days at a time and taking pounds of drugs, and hurled the glass pitcher at the wall, with his mind, of course. This really freaked me out. Eric was always a yeller, but he had never become violent and now I saw that he could very easily hurt me.

I started thinking to myself, I wish I could go back to before he even started messing with these drugs. I thought about the lab in the basement of the house we rented in North Hampton and that rainy Sunday, the day before St. Patrick's Day, when he had rushed upstairs and told me the news.

And then I was there, both upstairs watching a movie on the couch, and in the corner of his lab.

"What do you need, babe?" he asked. I shrugged, walked up to him, and gave him a hug and waked back upstairs to look at myself watching TV. I then thought about coming back home and BOOM, there I was. All of the color had drained out of Eric's face. He asked if I had just made myself invisible and I told him that I had gone back in time. I had only been gone a minute or so, but we started experimenting more and more. Or rather, I experimented, and he hung around back here, amazed but getting sickened by jealousy more and more every day.

You see, I would go and do things like visit my old elementary school during a field day and just watch how happy I was, or go even further back. I went to Woodstock - took some really cool video, too. I didn't try taking him with me until a few weeks later - he was adamant about staying back, in case something went wrong, but even if it did, what was he going to do? I finally convinced him to let me try and I took him back to the Duck Boat Parade for the 2007 Red Sox, but he didn't have a good time. His brain couldn't wrap around why I had the power and he didn't and what he and I should do with my power.

Oh, he listed all sorts of big things - save JFK, prevent 9/11, kill Hitler and tell Buckner to be super-careful in the ninth inning of Game 6 of the 86 World Series, but we couldn't really do any of that. Not only would we not have the kind of access to do those things, but we could seriously screw up the universe by doing some of that stuff. Those were major things with major implications. If we wanted to do things, they had to be small with infinitesimal chances of skewing the space-time continuum. In hindsight, everything you do in time is going to affect things, but I have grown very weary of pretending to care.

You see, Peter, this is my universe now. I have changed everything and I will continue to do so. I have an awesome power and I have no problem wielding it.

I wielded it on that little slut, Cassidy. That little bitch would have broken up my family - she did the first time through - but this time I bumped her off and my family stayed together forever. My Dad was her teacher and he couldn't keep it in his pants, OK, and she begged him for it - I saw her. I went back and watched. He didn't force it on her. She wanted it, until, of course she got pregnant. She was going to tell him about it the Monday after Halloween, but she didn't get the chance. And he didn't get the chance to kill her this time.

I know, I was really lucky my Dad wasn't still a suspect in her murder. I mean, he would have been the prime suspect if anybody knew about their illicit relationship, but Cassidy was a good little slut, who wanted my Dad to run away with her and leave his wife nine months pregnant and about to burst.

Not this time, bitch. I kept my Daddy safe and my family together. I'm a goddamn hero for traditional family values and all it cost me was murdering a pregnant teen slut.

No big loss for humanity, if you ask me.

My second victim was the brilliant one, though. No connection to her at all. Nobody really has any connection to her, because she's from the 17th century. I did my homework on her.

As you know, Cabot is very close to Salem, the city where all the witch trials went down. I went to the historical archives and did a ton of research, looking for a woman that the town was going to kill for being a witch that I could abduct and murder instead. I found the perfect victim - Alice Parker. They hung her on Sept. 22, so I stole her from her jail cell on Sept. 21, brought her back to Cabot and murdered her in the Enchanted Garden.

It is really throwing the cops off, I bet. They are sending her picture around the country right now trying to identify her and they never will. They're checking dental records, DNA, fingerprints, all that but it's like she doesn't even exist. It's keeping that stupid town shivering in their boots though. Hell, even now in 2035, The Cabot Butcher keeps kids up at night and has people looking over their shoulders when they're walking around at night.

The Cabot Butcher, meaning me, strikes several times a year in Cabot – always remembering certain anniversaries and trying to stay true to my initial victims. Promiscuous girls get axed on Halloween, drunks get sliced o St. Patty's Day and Cabot Homecoming is when I really shine.

Killing Alice was the most fun I had - not the murder, although that gets less messy and more fun each time, but the research and the dressing in period dress in case I do get stopped. And you should have seen poor Alice's face when I transported her to the 21st century. There were planes overhead and she could hear cars pass on the road up the hill. She thought she was in Hell and that I was the devil. It was really funny.

But, now I'm left with this big question - now what? I can keep murdering people in Cabot, but I have you now. I keep thinking there is something bigger that you and I can accomplish. And yes, Peter, you were my target all along. You see, in the initial run of events, you were back at the Clarion when my Dad was going through his murder trial. You followed it from start to finish, writing nearly a hundred articles about every aspect of the murder and the case. You even wrote a story about me, the little girl who was left behind, and on the 20th anniversary of the murder, you did another story about what had happened to the people involved in the case in the years since the murder.

I loved meeting and speaking with you Peter. You really blew me away and though there was 30 years between us, I could sense a connection. I could see the fire in your eyes - the same fire I see in my eyes when I look in the mirror. There's a hunger for danger and adventure in there and, well, loneliness, of course. I could see that you – the older you – was still hoping to accomplish something great. I wanted to help you.

Since I've received this ability, I've been playing with time to get you where you are today. I maneuvered everyone like pieces on a chess board to get Ken O'Donnell out of the way quicker, to get you back at the paper, to get the cops searching all over the place, to let them think they could trap me, to get them to use you as bait. It has taken hundreds of tries to get it just right and now you are here with me.

I have a lot to offer you, Peter. In addition to sharing my incredible gift and going anywhere in the world at anytime in history, I'll give you me.

She stopped talking and looked at Peter for an answer. He tried not to look as frightened as he felt. He swallowed a few times in an attempt to wet his lips and incredibly dry mouth. She noticed him struggle and moved the water to him.

If I say no, Peter thought, she will kill me. She has nothing to lose and she can undoubtedly try to convince me again. Maybe find me when I'm at rock bottom and offer me unlimited power. I would definitely have taken her offer last year. If I say yes, though, what I am agreeing to, Peter wondered. Will she make me complicit in her killing spree through history.

"What do you want from me, Beckett?" he asked.

"First, call me Becky. Beckett is the name on my birth certificate, but all the boys who called me that in school got a knee to the groin," she said with a giggle.

"O.K., Becky it is," he said. "But, what do you plan to do? Do you want me to murder people with you, because I don't have it in me."

"I just want to see the history of the world with you, experience everything and live beyond my wildest dreams," she said. "That doesn't have to involve murder, but if it does, so be it."

This woman had clearly lost her mind, but if he wanted to live, he had to play along, at least until he could find a way to stop her and or escape.

"Like vampires," she said.

"Huh?"

"The vampires in those Anne Rice novels, they were incredibly wealthy and that was because they could take what they wanted and live forever. We can live whenever. We could go back to when Coca-Cola stock hits the stock market, buy 10,000 shares and come back to today and be billionaires," she said, moving around the room excitedly, hoping to convince him.

"I want you to show me," he said. "But I don't want to kill anybody. That has to stop."

Becky's head sagged.

"I know. I got carried away by the power and I just wanted to keep my Dad out of jail, so I could get to know him outside of a crowded room in a prison," she said. "And that girl made me so angry. That one stab became two and then five and then ten. Then I got bored and decided to get creative and try to spin the web to get you."

"Well, you got me," Peter said. "But if this is ever going to work out, no more lies or traps."

Becky put on a sultry, seductive face and sat by his side.

"Even though you are trapped," she cooed, stroking his hair and his face. Peter was still immobile due to the sedatives and he wouldn't be able to get out of 2035 without her help.

Chapter 9

Then can I walk beside you
I have come here to lose the smog
And I feel to be a cog in something turning
Well maybe it is just the time of year
Or maybe it's the time of man
I don't know who I am
But you know life is for learning

"Woodstock" - Joni Mitchell

Kissing Becky was not unpleasurable. She was a beautiful woman and Peter was not feigning his excitement as their lips met, although he did have to try and push thoughts of her slicing through women with a knife far from his mind. He hadn't been with a woman in nearly two years and he found himself getting flushed as he and Becky ramped up their lovemaking. Whatever happened between them right now would not last long, and ironically, Peter was thankful. He didn't really want to have sex with this monster, but he also knew that right now he couldn't stop himself either.

After the act was over and Becky left the room to go and clean up, Peter found his thoughts drifting to Tracy, his last girlfriend. Their break-up came during his rocketing trip to rock bottom and it triggered an even more precipitous fall for Peter. When every fiber of his being was crying out for help, he pushed her away. There were a lot of tears in the final stages of that relationship, a time that dragged on for weeks and weeks, but unfortunately for Peter, and fortunately for Tracy who was happily married, never ended in a reconciliation.

He and Tracy had been together for three years but only the first half of the relationship could be considered any good and Peter could scarcely remember any of those moments any more. In the two years since they had broken up, Peter had desperately tried to reconnect with some of those good memories - her smile, their first kiss, sliding her clothes off on cold Sunday mornings in winter, but the memories were all tainted now. One good one inevitably led to several bad ones - times that Peter found himself screaming or Tracy crying.

Love is a vicious cycle, thought Peter. People fall in love with people who are bad for them, get hurt, and then do it all over again. Sometimes it is with the same person and other times the person finds that this time they are the bad person in a relationship.

Before Peter could get any more maudlin thinking about the girl who got away, the girl who wouldn't let him escape re-entered the room.

"O.K., Petey, when do you want to start?" she asked, bouncing around the room. He was finally starting to get use of his limbs back and sat up gingerly.

"No time like the present," he offered.

"You are a writer, aren't you?" she chuckled. "O.K., we can go on a trip today, but let's lay some ground rules first."

He nodded his head in agreement.

" Do not try to pass messages to anyone. Any, 'Help me I'm being held captive by a time traveling maniac' messages and I'll take you to the Jurassic period and feed you to a dinosaur or something equally mean and painful," Becky said in a warning tone.

"And if we travel to see a younger you in your past, you really better mind your P's and Q's, or I'll just kill your younger you right in front of yourself and watch you disintegrate."

Peter audibly gulped.

"That's right, baby. You should be scared of me. I can be a mean old mama," Becky said, sidling up close to him and nuzzling his ear. "But I can be nice, too."

"I got it, don't try anything funny," Peter said. "I won't try anything, Becky. I promise. I want to go in to this with an open mind. Few people ever get the chance to time travel, right?"

"Damn skippy, sweetie," she agreed, walking over to a pile of what Peter recognized as his clothes. She tossed him his jeans and a t-shirt and he slowly pulled them on.

"What are the other rules?" he asked, wincing as his muscles cramped at their first activity in god knew how long. Two days? 28 years?

"We're going to stay in the vicinity of the last 50 years - 1985-2035 - we won't be spotted as clearly from another time and place if we do that," she said and Peter thought this was extremely reasonable.

"Can we go anywhere in the world or do we have to stay in the geographical area of Cabot?" Peter asked.

"We can go anywhere, but if we're going some place I've never been, I need to get a very clear picture in my head," Becky explained. "The time I went to Woodstock, I ended up on stage during Jimi Hendrix's set, because that's the vision of Woodstock I had in my head. Luckily, everyone was so fucked up they didn't notice a girl just materializing out of thin air."

Peter laughed. He could imagine one of the few sober people at the show seeing Becky appear and trying to convince his stoned buddies about what he just saw.

"Also, time obviously still passes, right? How does this all work?" Peter asked.

"Look at you trying to get all brainy," Becky said, looking impressed. "You - current you - is living your life. You are here now, but your life-line is still the same. Although you are in 2035, your body is still aging as if it were back home. If we decide to live in the year 3000, which we won't do, because, ewww, barring any injuries or any accidental death, you would likely live until 3056."

"I want to see my death," Peter said.

"Honey, no," Becky begged.

"As it still stands, before we get too crazy with messing with the space-time thingamabob, I want to see my death at the age of, what, 79?"

Becky shook her head.

"You've already been there, haven't you?" Peter asked, knowing that if Becky was as obsessed with him as she claimed to be, and he had no reason to doubt her, she had likely seen him at the hospital as a baby and probably visited him as a visiting nun on his deathbed.

"Yeah, I have, but seeing your death isn't cool. We can go anywhere. You want to see the Berlin Wall come down? That's a good party," Becky offered.

"Why don't we just go for a walk right now - good old 2035?" Peter suggested. He didn't think the future would be all that different, but it was worth seeing, and it was a form of time travel, at least for him.

"I'd rather drive," she said, primping herself in the mirror. "I don't live in the best neighborhood. In fact, there might not even be a best neighborhood in Cabot now. Maybe just the best of the worst."

Peter noticed that Becky's eyes went flat as she talked about the current state of Cabot and wondered if she thought about being at least partly responsible for the town's demise. It wasn't as if Cabot had been this shining beacon on a hill in his time, but he had always felt safe. She exited the room and Peter slowly followed, getting his land legs back.

Becky drove a futuristic version of a Nissan hatchback. It was black with funky, Japanese images stenciled on the sides in red. It had a very sleek look and Peter guessed that it was probably very eco-friendly.

"This is kind of a throwback car," Becky explained. "A 2020 Nissan Seibu, but I'm kind of a traditionalist."

She pressed a button on her key chain and the gull wing doors on both the driver's side and passenger side flipped open. Music instantly blared out of the stereo and Peter recognized it as U2's "Where The Streets Have No Name."

"U2?" he said as a question, even though he knew the answer.

"I like the oldies," Becky said.

"So do I," Peter agreed, feeling very old that this album was considered an oldie.

The Seibu backed out of Becky's garage and Peter's tour around Cabot in the year 2035 began.

They passed a large, multi-leveled brick complex with dozens of athletic fields and parks on either side. Peter thought a college must have come to town, but he soon saw a sign reading "Richardville Elementary."

"That's Richardville Elementary?" he asked with a tone of disbelief.

Becky nodded and smiled.

"Yep, my alma mater. It's now a sleepover school and did you notice the gates? That's for safety. It just makes people feel better knowing their kids are safe inside their elementary school and other kids aren't bringing in things like guns and drugs."

Were kids bringing drugs and guns to elementary schools, Peter wondered. That was what was going to happen within 28 years?

Becky crested a hill and Peter looked to his right to see bumper to bumper traffic on the interstate below him.

"That's one thing that never changes," Peter said. "Traffic."

"It's like that almost 24-7," Becky said, tossing the remark off as if this kind of traffic was inevitable. Peter was growing more and more depressed by future Cabot and the trip had barely even begun.

The car trekked on its merry way past a Super Wal-Mart Shopping Center and only after Peter saw a sign for Lake Hammond a quarter of a mile past the mall did he realize that used to be the YMCA where he learned how to swim and attended day camp. He caught a hot sob in his throat.

"Are you O.K.?" Becky asked, turning to face him for a second to register his facial expression.

Peter nodded weakly and looked away. Of course this is what his town would look like in 28 years because that's the way he thought the world would look in the future. There were many other horrible sights during their hour long ride around Cabot, but Peter had detached himself from what he was seeing. Among the many general things he noticed were the number of houses that had been sandwiched into tiny parcels of land, spaces that used to be green space or someone's front yard.

There were also a lot of people milling about and none of their behavior looked particularly friendly.

"Those people are zombies," Becky said and Peter freaked out.

"Zombies?!?"

"Not real zombies, you goof. Zombies aren't real," Becky said, trying to reassure her guest from the past. "They're drug zombies. All hooked on a hallucinogen called Sunshine. It's good stuff, but it isn't real. I prefer reality to manufactured utopia."

Spoken like a person who can leave this hellhole whenever she likes, Peter thought to himself. He was very glad they weren't walking around the town because he would have been entirely too creeped out to walk past the Sunshine zombies.

"I've been off drugs, for the most part, since Eric gave me the shot," Becky said.

Peter closed his eyes for a minute and fantasized about drinking a large glass of whiskey.

Becky drove by the ocean and that's when Peter asked her to turn the car around. The water was cluttered with house boats and garbage. Cabot now looked like those scary pictures of harbors that you would sometimes see in the movies or issues of National Geographic.

"I want to go home," he said.

"Home to my house or home to your time?" she asked.

"I don't care," he said and it was true, he didn't care. He didn't see the point anymore. This Cabot, this world, looked inevitable and he was sure that he and the rest of humanity would glide right into it without realizing that everything was terribly wrong.

Becky turned the Seibu around and the trip back to her home was silent. She had shut off the music and kept glancing over at Peter but he just slumped in his seat and gazed out the window. She placed her hand on his knee and gave it a gentle rub and a shake but he didn't respond.

After returning to Becky's home, they climbed the stairs to her living room. Becky collapsed on her couch, while Peter paced slowly and aimlessly.

"You murdered people," he said softly.

"Not this again," she said, a little stung that he brought this up.

"You live in this fucked up world with a power to go back to the past and change things and yet all you did was act like Jason Voorhess or Michael Myers and chop people up," Peter yelled. "We have to change things!"

"What are we going to do, Peter? Go back in time and tell people to stop making babies, drive their cars less, stop littering in the ocean, don't take drugs?" Becky bellowed back. "Get fucking serious."

He was serious, but she was right. What good was her power when confronted with some serious global problems. He flopped back to the couch and sank into the cushions, completely dejected and worn out. It was funk of global proportions and the fact that he was stuck in the future with a psychopath just made it worse. At some point that day, Peter clicked off. He stopped caring, had to if he was going to survive, and Becky was right there waiting for him with her warm body, soft, inviting lips and that special power that could take them wherever they wanted to go.

Becky offered up suggestion after suggestion of places and times to visit over the next few days, but the only one that struck a chord with him was going to Woodstock.

Becky had been there before and now knew enough to not transport herself on to the stage.

She and Peter made tie-dye t-shirts the night before they were going to leave on their trip and, though he tried hard not to, Peter had fun. Becky fired up a small grill in her back yard to cook some steaks and the two of them killed a bottle of wine. Peter figured 28 years of sobriety was long enough. The tipsy couple giggled while dipping white t-shirts, wrapped tight with rubber bands and stencils, into pails of colorful dyes. After a few dunks in other pails, Becky placed her shirt in a pail of bright red dye. She removed her hand and slapped it in the middle of Peter's t-shirt, leaving a dripping wet, red hand print. He squirmed away from her and when she stopped giving chase seconds later, he dipped his hands in the green dye and grabbed her by the seat of her pants. She turned to him, her mouth slightly open, and bent in for a kiss.

The next day, clad in their homemade hippie gear, Becky and Peter stood in the middle of her backyard.

"So, how does this work? What do I have to do?" Peter asked.

"Just hold my hands and look pretty," she said, taking hold of both of his hands and closing her eyes.

"Should I close my eyes too?" he asked her earnestly.

"I always do, but that's just so I can visualize where I am going," she explained. "Maybe you should keep your eyes open so that you can tell me what time travel looks like."

Peter considered her suggestion, but worried that what he saw in that span might fry his brain and drive him crazy. He then decided he didn't care if he fried his brain and went crazy. At least then he wouldn't be carrying around the guilt of shacking up with The Cabot Butcher.

"Are you doing it now?" he asked. "How will I know when you're doing it?"

She shushed him and he quieted down, not wanting to screw anything up and possibly get abandoned at some unknown point in history.

Peter stared at Becky, who was concentrating very hard on getting them to a piece of the land where Woodstock took place, and he tried to imagine what her brain was doing that could produce such an amazing miracle. Out of the corner of his eye, Peter could swear he saw the trees in Becky's backyard wiggle. After that, it seemed like things got intensely bright, as if the sun had become a spotlight and it was whiting out the yard and everything in it. A religious person would think it was the beginning of the rapture, but Peter saw it as Becky opening a time portal and moving them through. Peter kept his eyes open, at least as much as he could without going blind, but he didn't see much. Part of him expected to see ticking clocks or old women in rocking chairs float by, but it really was more of a nothingness.

And then they were there. Woodstock.

Peter practically wept at the fresh air and lack of dirt and grime. Yes, it was crowded and it was raining a little, but it just felt good to be out in the country and around people with good vibes. Everywhere he looked he saw a mass of people in brightly colored tops and lots and lots of denim. Looking towards the stage, he saw gigantic metal towers springing up from the ground, like machines out of an H.G. Wells novel.

The rambling boogie of "Going Up The Country" by Canned Heat was pumping out through the crowd, which meant that they had arrived late Saturday afternoon. He had done some studying of the event before the left 2035 and he knew that he was going to get to see The Who - if he could stay awake that long.

"Come on," Becky said pulling him through the throng of dancing, writhing people and clouds of skunky smelling marijuana smoke. Peter had a feeling he was going off the "no pot smoking wagon" this weekend too and he didn't really care. Becky stopped them when they had a good enough view of the stage and enough room to dance around and move their arms. People checked them out when they had stopped and, though they definitely looked older than most of the people attending the festival, several of the guys were checking Becky out and nodding their approval at Peter.

Canned Heat was playing an excellent instrumental jam and people were clapping during a slow part that blended into a piece of music that Peter felt sounded like gospel. They sang of sunshine, and although it was overcast, Peter could feel it warming him. He looked at the lead singer with his bushy black beard and yellow shirt and just felt happy. The man hugged a young man in a blue t-shirt that jumped on stage during a jam that featured part of "Crossroads" and even lit his cigarette.

Someone tapped Peter's shoulder and passed a joint to him. Peter gave him the "much obliged" tip of the joint and took a few drags before offering to pass it back. The man shook his head and smiled and Peter was officially getting high for the first time in months - 66 years if you wanted to be technical about it. He caught Becky's eye as she was grooving to the music and she smiled at him. He offered the joint to her, but she shook her head. Although she was beginning to trust Peter more and more, Peter knew she was not going to allow herself to get clouded by drugs and let him get a step ahead of her. He thought about this for an instant and it brought a storm of anger to the front of his mind. He decided to push it away though and enjoy the day.

Canned Heat finished their set and thanked the crowd and Peter saluted them back with a hearty "woo-hoo." Having not been born when Woodstock happened, he couldn't believe his fortune to be here, witnessing one of the greatest moments in rock and roll history. He was going to get to see amazing things tonight and tomorrow and he had a crazy woman named Becky to thank for it. He turned to her and gave her a hug and she turned that moment into a long-lasting kiss.

The rest of the evening became a repetitive blur of pot-smoking, booze drinking, light petting and rocking out. Peter and Becky watched Janis Joplin strut her stuff with her beautifully abrasive vocals, saw what could only be described as a strange, glitch-filled set by Grateful Dead, sang along with Creedence Clearwater Revival, danced in the early hours of Sunday morning to Sly and the Family Stone and then watched The Who blast their way to a zenith in the pantheon of great rock and roll performances.

The Who had toured during Peter's lifetime as an adult, but Peter never went because he felt that it just wouldn't be the same. Seeing them in their prime and hearing them play "Tommy" was incredible. He had mostly sobered up by then, but he was exhausted, kept awake and thrumming only by the music that was blasting and the experience of seeing the original line-up of The Who.

And yet, there was a feeling of being watched that Peter couldn't shake. He had felt it several times earlier in the day but just chalked it up to drug-induced paranoia. In his stoner days, he often felt like the pizza delivery guys were working for the cops and were trying to sniff out marijuana or anything fishy going on when they came to the door. The feeling he got today was not like that at all. It was more like someone was staring at him, someone he could see in the periphery of his vision, but was gone when he turned his head to stare.

Becky didn't seem to notice and, if she did, she didn't seem to care. To all the hippies around them, Peter just looked like another paranoid head, if they even took any notice. Like he did earlier in the day, Peter just pushed the thoughts out of his mind and focused on the music.

When The Who finished, playing out the last notes of "Naked Eye," Peter, like many in the crowd crashed and Becky was close behind him. The two kept their spots and slept against each other. It wasn't the cleanest thing in the world and they were a little chilled by the moisture filled air that morning, but they were so tired it didn't really matter very much at all.

There weren't as many people around them as there were earlier and those that had remained were either asleep, passed out or stoned, oblivious to the goings on around them. If anyone saw the two large men approach the slumbering Peter and Becky, they thought nothing of it when all four of them disappeared in the blink of an eye.

Chapter 10

And when I'm lying in my bed
I think about life
And I think about death
And neither one particularly appeals to me
And if the day came when I felt a
Natural emotion
I'd get such a shock I'd probably lie
In the middle of the street and die
I'd lie down and die ..

"Nowhere Fast" - The Smiths

    Peter woke up in a gasping panic, breathless and completely unaware of his surroundings. He still dreamt as if he were in his own time, but part of his brain was searching for the cramped, damp surroundings of Sunday morning at Woodstock. He was also looking for Becky, making sure she hadn't stranded him some place far from home so that she could continue to murder and haunt their hometown.

    His eyes, opened wide and rapidly searching for anything familiar, did not recognize where he was, but he felt that he was in another type of hospital or institution. Perhaps he had just gone crazy and all of this time traveling and sex with a time traveling serial killer was just a figment of his imagination. Peter did not see Becky, so it was possible that he had dreamt it all, and yet he didn't feel as if his brain had slipped a cog.

    As he caught his breath and slowed his heart to a normal pace, he started to try to figure out where, and when, he was. It did appear that he was in a hospital. Everything looked very standard and sterile, from his bed with crisp, folded sheets to the box of tissues on the waist high dresser and the small bathroom with an almost brand new looking toilet and shower. He most certainly was not in the 1960s, because the equipment in the room was too modern, but it was not so futuristic looking that he couldn't tell what did what, so the possibility of being in the far future wasn't likely either. It appeared that he was back in the 21st century, either in his time or close enough.

    If there were only a television in the room, he could tell for sure. Was "Jeopardy" still on? How old does Alex Trebek look? Who's playing for what teams on the highlights on "SportsCenter"?

    Peter's clothes had been removed and replaced with light blue, cotton pajamas. He felt a little like Dick Van Dyke on his old show with Mary Tyler Moore. He would have felt even more like old Dick if Becky were lying in a separate bed next to him.

    Her absence did worry him. Not only could it mean that he was stranded somewhere he didn't want to be stranded, but it could also mean that she was somewhere looking for him, livid that he got away and a second from going into Peter's past and wiping him off the planet. He was very frightened of Becky, despite the fact that he had allowed himself to have sex with her and had even enjoyed it and made it enjoyable for her. He felt like a victim of domestic abuse, afraid that no matter where he was or what he was doing (just sitting in a hospital, minding his own business), he was doing something wrong and she was going to find out, get really angry and put a severe, perhaps even fatal, hurting on him.

Peter debated trying to run. This room could be a trap or a prison of some sort, but so was staying with Becky. He was sure there were worse fates than being stuck with a female slasher, but he did not think he would be so unlucky as to go from bad to worse.

He began to rub the tops of his fingers and the knuckles on each of his hands, a nervous habit he had picked up at some point over the last few years, and thought about who he would see come through that door in the next few minutes. It could be Becky, here to either rescue him or slice him into several pieces, or it could be someone new, someone who could protect him, right the world and take him home.

Neither option turned out to be correct.

A small, dark haired older woman timidly entered the room trailing a small rolling table with a tray of food on it. She didn't say anything and Peter did not try to coax her into a conversation. He just gave a brief nod of thanks before lifting the plastic dome off the food and eating what looked like a fairly generic chicken dinner, complete with a scoop of mashed potatoes, brightly colored green beans and carrots and a roll smeared with a brush stroke of melted butter. He also drank a carton of milk, neglecting to search for an expiration date to place when he was, and a cup of coffee in a plastic brown mug.

He pushed the tray aside when he was finished and let his head fall back to the pillows. He was not tired, per se, but the last few weeks of his life had exhausted him. He closed his eyes and let his mind touch upon all of the places he had been and the things he had done.

Peter was unsure of how much time had passed when the door to his room had finally opened again. It was not the small, silent older woman, but a tall, serious looking man in a navy blue suit. The man was in his late 40s or early 50s, with a severe receding hairline and had a tightly clipped dark moustache. He had an air of military authority about him and Peter was immediately intimidated and ready to salute.

"Peter, my name is Frank Walker. We have a lot to do and very little time to do it in," he said. "Please come with me."

Peter started to get out of bed, but hesitated.

"Will you at least tell me where I am?" Peter asked, in something resembling a whine.

"You are in an underground bunker in Langley, Virginia," Walker said.

"You're CIA?" Peter said with a hint of surprise, although Walker looked like every Fed that Peter had ever seen in the movies or on TV.

"Not exactly, but I'll explain it on the way," Walker said, ushering him out of the room and into an expansive, neon-lit hallway. Peter was wearing a pair of thin, papery slippers with a sticky gripped bottom, so his feet groaned against the floor, while Walker's heavy and heavily polished, black, loafers pounded the floor and echoed, announcing their presence around every corner.

"I work for an International Security Consortium concerned with universal spatial interruption," Walker said, pausing for a moment to look at Peter when he didn't respond. "Time crime," he explained, before starting up his rapid march once again.

"I'm sorry," Peter said, pleading for mercy. "I had no idea that going to Woodstock would ruin the universe."

"It's not you, Peter, it's her," Walker stated. "Beckett Glidden."

"Where is she?" Peter asked, part of him hoping that they had destroyed her and the other part of him hoping she was still alive.

"She's here," Walker stated matter of factly. "She is heavily sedated and under 24 hour armed surveillance."

"Are you going to kill her?" Peter asked.

Walker looked like he was seriously thinking about it, even going so far as to pucker his lips and cast his gaze upwards, looking for answers.

"No," he said finally. "Miss Glidden is much too valuable for us to do that."

"But she's a psychotic maniac," Peter said.

"Oh, we may never get to work with her directly, but her brain is of exceptional interest to our researchers. She is one of the first time travelers on record after all," Walker said almost reverently.

"No. I didn't know that," Peter quietly admitted.

"There's a lot you don't know, Peter, and we'll try to catch you up as quick as we can," Walker said. "There is a lot of work to be done and you will be instrumental in helping us achieve our goals."

"I'll do what I can," said Peter. Walker clapped him on the shoulder with a solid hand, smiled, and began to walk rapidly once again towards a destination that was apparently very far away from Peter's room.

Peter wondered how he could possibly help a government agency, aside from ratting out past associates in seedy underbelly of the Cabot drug scene. He didn't even know that much about Becky, other than what she had told him about her boyfriend and his experiments with mind chemistry.

Walker stopped at a door and ran a plastic card through a card reader. The door opened and he motioned for Peter to follow him.

It was a conference room with several people sitting in plush, leather seats. There was a spot open at the head of table, presumably for Walker, and a seat to the right of his that Peter expected was meant for him. There were three video monitors on the wall and the pictures on them changed every 10-15 seconds. Peter saw Becky in one of them. She was asleep, possibly unconscious, and bound by her arms and legs to a stretcher. Peter couldn't tell what the other pictures on the screens were. They were outside scenes and Peter expected they were from security cameras focused on the perimeter of the building.

"Let's begin," Walker announced. "Agent Stafford, please give us an update on Miss Glidden."

A bespectacled, middle age man with wild hair shuffled some notes and began speaking.

"Beckett Glidden, a 28 year old female from the year 2035, is in our custody. She is being heavily sedated with 300 milligrams of Tornex and she is under both leg and arm restraints. She is to be considered armed and dangerous and must be under 24 hour armed surveillance until further notice," Stafford said, pausing to accentuate the importance of his statement.

"Continue," Walker said, motioning with his hand for Agent Stafford to pick up the pace.

"While here, we plan to do a number of tests and exams on her brain activity. She is considered to be the mother of time travel and we feel that the educational possibilities she can provide us alive are far more important, right now, than the security benefits of destroying her immediately," Stafford said. A man in a military uniform stood up to chime in his two cents.

"Director Walker, I must disagree with this Agent Stafford's assessment, sir. Beckett Glidden is the most prolific serial killer in the human race's entire history. She needs to be eliminated immediately and we must try to go back and repair the damage."

Peter's eyes widened at the military man said that Beckett was the most prolific serial killer.

"Excuse me," Peter muttered before clearing his throat and continuing. "I think she has only killed two people. I know that's bad, but, that's not hundreds or anything."

The military man looked at Walker for approval to say something and received a brief nod.

"Mr. Miller, Beckett Glidden has murdered 8,000 people over the span of 600 years that we know of. She has used her amazing power for unspeakable evil. This department, after finally cracking the code for time travel 12 years ago, was created solely for the purpose of attempting to right her wrongs," the military man said, turning to the rest of the people at the table. "That's why we can't afford to take any chances with her. We need to kill her now."

It appeared as though most of the people in the conference room. including Peter, were swayed by that argument. Peter even began to nod.

"No, I'm sorry, but we are keeping Miss Glidden alive, at least for the time being," Walker said. "I believe I have a better idea of how to stop her and possibly fix the past and it revolves around Mr. Miller here."

Peter turned and gave a shocked look to Walker.

"Hear me out, Peter. I think you'll find that you are our best hope," Walker said. "Let me explain."

The plan involved a lot of trickery, double-crossing and secrecy, but Peter had to admit it had its merits. If it all went off without a hitch.

The agency had developed a form of time travel that relied on similar principles to the way Becky traveled through time. The difference was Becky's time travel occurred internally, somewhere in her brain, while the agency's occurred through a small microchip that stimulated the same part of the brain externally. The agency would give the power to Peter, teach him how to use it, and then allow Becky to think she escaped and rescued Peter who was being tortured for information. She would likely flee with Peter back to her home and that was when Peter would get down to business.

It would be up to him to convince her that he was now solidly an ally and that they needed to go back to her ex-boyfriend's lab, make sure she still got her power and try to get a power from the injection for Peter as well. This would lead the agency to the exact time and place where Becky first got her power. Once at the lab, the agency would spring into action. They would re-capture Becky, destroy the chemical concoction and not have to attempt to fix history piece by piece.

Basically, stop Becky from getting the ability to time travel and save the world.

"Why haven't you already done this?" Peter asked.

"We don't know when or where this happened," Walker said.

"What about going back and killing her before she became a time traveler?" Peter asked.

Agent Stafford answered Peter's question.

"Mr. Miller, we don't want to kill Miss Glidden. We feel that she could be a great asset to us - with the proper training and conditioning, of course."

Walker nodded, motioned for Agent Stafford to stop talking and began to speak himself.

"Peter, Miss Glidden can do amazing things. It has taken us centuries to even come close to her abilities," Walker said and Peter's eyes went wide again.

"Centuries? Just what year are we in here anyway?" Peter asked, moderately annoyed.

"2517," Walker said.

"Jesus," Peter said, stunned that there was a 2517, given the way things were going in 2035.

"There is a lot we don't know about time travel and how things work," Walker admitted. "We want to be careful and make sure that the moves we make are the right ones. If we kill her..."

"You may not ever invent time travel," Peter said. He didn't like it, but he understood. Becky had apparently done so much killing, that no one could even say what effect each murder had on the world. Killing the mother of time travel could possibly do even more damage than they cared to think about.

"She is a horrible person, Peter, but she has the ability to do great things," Walker said. "We need to hold on to that potential and try to use it to the benefit of humanity as long as possible."

Peter accepted this explanation and Walker's sincerity and the rest of the meeting was spent planting the chip on and in Peter's skull.

"This is going to sting a little," Walker said. Peter closed his eyes and braced himself for a pinch. It was much worse than that.

To make it look like he had been beaten and not planted with a homing device, an armed soldier cracked Peter on the forehead with the butt of his gun and opened up a small wound. The strike knocked Peter unconscious and while he was out, a nurse cleaned the wound and stuck the chip in. She then dressed the wound with a healthy helping of gauze and ran some smelling salts beneath Peter's nostrils to rouse him.

Peter's eyes fluttered for a moment before opening wide and looking angry. He grabbed for his forehead and winced.

"What the fuck?" he yelled.

"We have to make this look official," Walker said. "If she thinks anything funny is going on, your life could be in danger."

"Don't you think cracking me in the skull is kind of putting my life in danger?" Peter asked.

"Gramercy here is a professional," Walker said with a hint of a smile. "Let's go try out your new toy."

Walker started to exit the room and Peter slowly got to his feet and followed him. He felt bone-tired and completely mistreated. Wasn't it just a short time ago that he had nothing specific to do all day but write his never-ending novel and dream about getting wasted? He had hoped for a kick-start to his life, something to rouse and shake him from years of slothfulness, but now he craved a moment of peace. Just a minute where the fate of the world didn't hang in the balance.

In some respects, it felt great to be useful and wanted but there was a niggling little thought that kept increasing its volume in the back of his head, reminding him that Peter Miller was the last person anyone should trust with the fate of the world.

Chapter 11

Go on, go on scream and cry
You're miles from where anyone will find you
This is nothing new, no television crew
They don't even put on the sirens

"Star Witness" - Neko Case

Detective Chris Leonard pulled his SUV into a parking space in front of The Cabot Clarion, removed his "Big One" coffee from Dunkin Donuts from the cup holder, exited the car and quickly walked into the newspaper's offices. It was a very cold day, as November days in Massachusetts tend to be, and Leonard did not want to spend any more time outside than was necessary. He had already given himself a pretty bad cold from wearing himself down by pounding the streets day and night looking for signs of the killer who may or may not have abducted Peter Miller over a week ago. He looked pale, withdrawn and exhausted.

"How are you, Detective?" Nancy asked upon seeing them, although the answer was all over his face. "Go on up."

She buzzed Jerry Jackson's office and told him the detective was on his way up. Leonard went up the stairs and hung a left, tapping a brief knock on Jerry's door.

"Come on in, Chris," Jerry said, rising to shake the detective's hand before sitting again and offering Leonard a seat. "Any news?"

Leonard shook his head. There hadn't been a murder, at least one they discovered, since the found the body of the police officer who had been tasked with trailing Peter as he drove to the fake arrest house. Leonard knew that Jerry was really asking if there was any news on Peter Miller, his reporter, who had been missing since shortly after posting a not entirely true story about an imminent arrest of a murder suspect.

It had been fairly quiet since the day of the fake arrest. No bodies had been discovered and the newspaper hadn't received any more letters from Beckett Glidden, the alleged name of the murderer.

"I was actually dropping by to see if you had heard anything," Leonard said. The detective was weighed down with guilt. He knew that he and Chief Woodfin had pushed Peter into acting as bait, but he never in his worst nightmares expected what had happened to happen.

On the morning of the ill-fated chase, Leonard and several members of the Cabot police department sat at the ready in the arrest house in direct communication with Officer Graboski, the officer they had placed in the parking lot close to the Cabot Clarion. Graboski was tasked with following Peter to the arrest house in the hopes that the killer would be following Peter. Somewhere between 9:30 and 10 a.m. that morning, Graboski had been murdered in the parking lot. His throat had been slashed and the killer, this monster Glidden, had kept Graboski upright so that no one had noticed anything was wrong, until Leonard tried to contact him to leave the parking lot and start the trail.

By then it was too late.

Approximately a quarter-mile from the arrest house, Peter's car was side-swiped by another car. It had rolled over several times and was completely totaled. Leonard

believed that Glidden was behind the wheel of the car that hit Peter's, but how he could have possibly known
where Peter had been driving to was beyond him. A part of him wanted to accuse someone on the force of acting in collusion with Glidden, but only a few people were in on the plan and none of them could have done something so horrible.

Perhaps the thing that surprised Leonard the most was the fact that both cars were still at the scene of the accident but both Miller and Glidden were gone from the scene and nowhere to be found within minutes of the crash. Leonard thought that somebody had to have been helping Glidden, even if it was just to give him and his victim a ride somewhere, but there was nothing.

One minute they were there and the next they weren't.

"We've put stories both in our paper and our web site, pleading for any information on the murders or Peter's whereabouts," Jerry said. "Other than more than a few people speculating that he is in some gutter, dive bar, brothel or crack house, we haven't heard anything."

"He certainly left a mark on some people," Leonard said smiling. "But, there is no way he is just hiding out somewhere. That sick fucker Glidden has him."

"And what do you think that means for our friend, Peter," Jerry said sadly.

"Nothing good," Leonard admitted. "But until we hear differently, there's always hope."

The men nodded, but if hope were oxygen, the lack of hope in the room would have left both of the men dead on the floor.

Despite the staff's feelings about Peter, they were hurt by his absence. They did not know of his plan with the police until later that afternoon, when Leonard came by and told them the story of how everything went wrong. Hillary sobbed a little bit that afternoon and her co-workers had heard those barely suppressed sobs at some point each work day over the past week. Hillary had certainly had her share of drama with Peter in the past, but she didn't want him dead and that was what he most certainly was, as far as anyone at the Clarion knew.

And yet, at 2:42 p.m., Tuesday, Nov. 11, 2007, Peter Miller was at his desk. It happened in a flash, although there was no flash, explosion or smoke. Peter was in the 26th century seconds earlier, chip in his head, visualizing the offices of the Cabot Clarion and his desk and right after thinking the word 'Go,' Peter had gone and was there. As his arrival made no noise, Hillary and Sam, both sitting across the room and not visible from Peter's desk, continued working on their computers. When Peter realized his trip had been a success, he did let out a bit of what could be called a whooping laugh.

Hillary jumped up from her seat and bolted over to Peter's desk.

"Peter?" she questioned, not sure if what she was seeing was really her co-worker or a ghost. Sam had followed cautiously behind her, fearing that Peter was here to wreak havoc from beyond the grave.

Peter stood up an nodded and Hillary rushed into his arms and gave him a hug, before stepping back seconds later.

"Where the hell have you been? How did you get here?"

Hillary continued to pepper Peter with questions, each one getting louder as Peter just kept shaking his head and laughing. Traveling 500 years into the past in the blink of an eye will do that to a person. The commotion brought Jerry and Detective Leonard out of Jerry's office and into the room. As Jerry saw Peter he rushed to him and enveloped him in a gigantic bear hug.

"Where have you been? Are you O.K.?"

"I'm fine," Peter said. He looked at Detective Leonard, who viewed him with a shocked expression and a little impatience, as if to ask why Peter hadn't come directly to him to help lead him to the killer, and nodded his head. Yes, Peter had a lot to tell Leonard, but he also did not have a lot of time to stay.

Peter and the agency had decided that he could tell the time travel story to whoever was around. They weren't likely to believe it, but if all went according to plan, the original way things happened would be restored and Peter would never be abducted by Becky in the first place, which would mean he would never get the time travel ability. There had been a lot of talk like that in his preparations with the agency, but Peter had started to tune it all out. It gave him a headache, all he wanted to know was that they had a plan for getting his life back to normal.

Peter laid out the story and no one at the Clarion believed him.

"You must still be in shock from your accident," Hillary said with a touch of concern that Peter did not fail to notice.

Sam quickly agreed with her and recounted a story about people who got severe cases of amnesia for weeks and months after traumatic accidents and then suddenly found themselves remembering everything and living their lives as is nothing had ever happened.

"Peter must have just snapped to earlier today, walked in and just come to his desk," Sam said. Peter did not have time to argue and knew it wouldn't have done him much good anyway.

"I hate to break up the welcome party, but I've got to bring Peter in and de-brief him," Leonard said.

"I've missed you, too, Chris, but I'd like to keep my pants on, if it's all the same to you," Peter said, definitely feeling more like himself than he had in months.

"Very funny," Leonard said.

"You'll be back tomorrow?" Jerry asked.

"Hopefully," Peter replied, thinking that if everything went according to plan, he may not be back here at all because Ken O'Donnell would never have left.

Peter and Leonard started heading towards the stairs, but Hillary stopped them with a question.

"Are we safe, Peter? Is the killer gone?"

Peter stared at Hillary and she had never looked more beautiful and fragile. He couldn't tell her the truth, which was that he simply didn't know, so he smiled and fell back on one of his most trusted skills, the ability to tell a white lie.

"Everyone is safe," he said. " 'The Butcher' won't be coming back."

Hillary smiled and Peter thought he could see a blush come to her cheeks.

As Peter and Leonard exited the building and walked to the doors of the SUV, Leonard asked Peter if what he had just said was true.

"I hope so," Peter said. "It better be."

Leonard started the SUV, backed out of the space and started driving.

"You're serious about all of this time travel shit, aren't you?" he asked.

"Absolutely," Peter said. "I know it sounds crazy, but that's why you can't identify the second victim, that's why you can't find a Beckett Glidden and that's how she and I left the scene of the accident so quick."

"I can't believe Beckett is a girl's name," Leonard said, shaking his head. "Red Sox fans are fucking nuts."

The two men shared a laugh as the vehicle proceeded up the road past a Dairy Queen boarded up for the winter. Leonard continued to drive in the opposite direction from the police station. Here was as good a place to talk as any and he had the feeling that Peter would not be staying long.

"So what's the plan?" Leonard asked, breaking the silence. "There is a plan to stop this crazy bitch, right?"

Peter took a deep breath. There was a plan, but Peter was thinking of putting his own spin on it. It wasn't that he didn't trust the agency, but he knew things could go wrong and he wanted to be prepared.

The chip that Peter had in his head also acted as a homing device. This was useful because not only could it be used to bring Peter back to the agency's safe room immediately in the case of an emergency, but it would act as a locator when he and Becky "broke out" of the agency. They wanted Peter to leave with her and convince her to take him to her boyfriend's lab so that he could be injected with the trigger serum as well.

Peter decided he would do this. The agency needed the serum and he would help them find it, but after that he was going to go and stop Becky from murdering Cassidy Samuels. If that meant killing her, so be it. Cabot would suffer too much if her murders were allowed to go unchecked. What Peter needed from Leonard was a diversion and to do that they needed to go back to Halloween day and put some things in motion.

Things were getting very complex and Peter's head was swimming as it thought about possible ramifications of every action he considered. It was like playing a very large game of chess (a game he was never particularly good at) with life or death consequences.

"Chris, I need you to pull the car over and be prepared to trust me implicitly and do everything I say," Peter said, taking note of the time on the glowing light of the radio. "I promise we'll be right back."

Leonard pulled the car over and Peter grabbed his hands. Leonard closed his eyes after he saw that Peter had done the same, even though he felt very silly and a little gay. Peter thought about his apartment on the day of Halloween, picturing the litter of notebook paper on the floor of his cluttered office and the television playing the "Friday the 13th" marathon all day. When he felt like he had the right place and the right time, Oct. 31, 11 a.m., he said "Go," unsure if he said it aloud or though it, and they were gone in a flash and there in an even briefer flash.

"Holy shit!" Leonard screamed. Peter put a finger to his lips, gesturing for him to be quiet.

"Shh, I'm asleep," he said, pointing to a room across the hall. Leonard looked confused and peeked his head into the room. He saw Peter sleeping soundly in a heap on the spectacularly unmade bed.

"This is so trippy," Leonard said. Peter nodded.

"We don't have much time. The agency is watching my location and if they think I'm going against them in any way, they could yank me back," Peter said.

"O.K., so what do we have to do?" Leonard asked.

"Just enough to mess up the day a little," Peter said with a smile.

Peter had Leonard call Cabot High School and leave a message for Becky's dad on his office voice mail.

"Mr. Glidden, this is Detective Chris Leonard from the Cabot Police Department. I am calling to urge you to cease any improper relationships you might be having. It is no longer a secret. If you would like to keep it from your family, friends and co-workers, you should no longer speak to any student outside of the classroom. I will be checking up on you in the coming days, so I recommend being on your best behavior."

Leonard hung up.

"What was that about?" he asked Peter.

"He kills Cassidy if Becky doesn't," explained Peter. "Or at least he did or will. Now, maybe he won't."

Leonard just shook his head a little bit.

"Now what?"

"I need you to post officers from the movie theater to the high school from as early as 10 p.m. to at least 7 a.m.," Peter said. "Becky said she followed Cassidy home from a party and nabbed her by the theater. If we change that path, who knows what else we might change."

Leonard nodded excitedly, thinking that this could work.

He placed a call to dispatch and put in an order for extra vehicles to patrol the area between the theater and the school from 10 a.m. until shift change.

His brow crinkled with worry.

"Wait a minute, if this is going to work, wouldn't it have already worked?"

"Huh?" asked Peter.

"Well, I mean, we just changed things in the past, so, shouldn't we know, like automatically know if we actually changed things?" Leonard said. Peter knew what Leonard was saying, or trying to say, but he had no answer so he just shrugged.

"Come on, let's get out of here before I wake up," Peter said, motioning with his head towards the sleeping past version of himself.

Peter once again held out his hands and closed his eyes, thinking about returning to Leonard's SUV. The chip that the agency had planted in him had something like a built in memory, so he didn't have to be super-specific. Leonard placed his hands on top of Peter's and they zoomed back to the present.

"Thanks for your help, Chris," Peter said. "We'll see if -"

Peter did not get to finish his sentence before being whisked back to the 26th century.

Chapter 12

The gallows shadows shook the evening,
In the night a hound dog bayed,
In the night the grounds were groanin',
In the night the price was paid.

"Seven Curses" - Bob Dylan

The agency was not pleased with Peter's deviation in plans. They made this abundantly clear by hitting him with a taser-like contraption immediately upon his return. Peter convulsed and grimaced in pain, his teeth clenched tightly and creating a creepy looking grin on his face.

Agent Walker looked down on Peter while he shook.

"Mr. Miller, you were only supposed to go back to one time destination and you went to two," Walker admonished. "We can't trust you or your motives."

Walker gave a signal to a member of the security team who promptly kicked Peter in the ribs and stepped on his right hand.

The air rushed out of Peter's lungs as Peter let out a yelp of pain at his throbbing fingers.

"Who did you talk to and what did you do?" Walker asked, not expecting Peter to talk and relishing the fact that this beating would go on a little longer at least.

Peter wasn't crying, but he blinked back some tears.

"I went back to my apartment on Halloween and put some extra food in my cat's dish," Peter said. "That's all."

Walker shook his head.

"We know someone went with you, Peter. Was it your cop friend, Detective Leonard?"

"No," Peter exclaimed. "I swear. I went alone."

Walker stood up straight, flattened out his jacket and addressed the members of the security team.

"He's not ready to cooperate with us. You have my permission to beat him within an inch of his life," Walker stated, as if he were granting permission to children to have a cookie. He turned around and exited the room and the beating really began.

The guard who had kicked him in the ribs earlier, picked him up and held him so that he would remain in a standing position while the other two guards cocked their arms back and swung at his face.

Peter debated whether this was real retaliation for violating their orders or if all of this was for show. It certainly felt like a vengeful ass kicking and it continued for several minutes. One guard would work on his body, punching at and below his gut, while another would step in and go at his face. The three guards rotated positions until they got bored and Peter was barely clinging to consciousness.

Before they exited the room, one of the now very sweaty and smelly guards stooped down and whispered in his ear.

"It hurts like a bitch right now, but you'll heal pretty fast. Don't worry, we've still got your back," he said placing his foot on the back of Peter's head and shoving it to the hard floor.

Walker was viewing the beating from Becky's cell. They had roused her from her drug-induced slumber before Walker had left Peter's room and had turned the television screen on so she could watch the violent scene.

"Who are you people and where the fuck am I?" Becky roared, straining against her restraints.

"We are the ones in control of the situation here and we are the ones asking questions," Walker responded.

Becky closed her eyes and tried to focus enough to zap herself somewhere else, somewhere safe.

"That won't work, Miss Glidden. Those restraints are emitting just enough of an electric current to disrupt your brain waves. You aren't traveling out of here anytime soon," Walker said, smug with victory. Becky had already decided he would die first and it would be soon and very, very painful and messy.

"You can leave him alone," Becky said, pointing her head towards the screen, which still showed Peter getting beaten. "He has no power and he doesn't know anything."

"I don't believe you," Walker said.

"It's true," she responded, still trying to get any kind of play in those itchy, tight straps that kept her arms pinned down.

"Well, I don't take the word of psychotic killers. I'm sorry," Walker roared.

Becky smiled.

"This isn't fair," she said with a hint of a smirk. "You know all about me, but I know nothing about you."

"Oh, Ms. Glidden, we're big fans of yours," Walker said.

"Of course, you are," Becky stated, as if everyone in the world felt the same way." But all my fans should know that the guy being beaten in that room is just a pawn."

Walker nodded.

"We do know that," he said. "But you'd be amazed at what kind of things we were able to get out of him. Things even he didn't realize he knew about you."

"Like what," Becky asked, sensing a bluff, but not wanting to blunder into a mistake.

"Come now, Miss Glidden, if you're smart enough to not give up the information we're looking for, even after hours of intense hypnotherapy, surely, we're smart enough to not give up our secrets," Walker said.

Had they given her hypnotherapy, Becky wondered. She couldn't remember anything about her time here, wherever she was.

"Your boyfriend in there isn't as strong as you though," Walker added. "We'll crack him soon and we'll find out the secret to his 'trigger serum,' I think he calls it."

Becky stifled a laugh. These assholes thought Peter was her scientist ex-boyfriend, Eric, the creator of the serum that gave her the power to time travel. Peter had obviously cracked enough to tell them about her power and how she got it, but he didn't know how or when to find it.

"Don't I get a phone call?" Becky asked.

"That law doesn't exist here," Walker said, standing up and turning off the television.

"Where am I, exactly? Guantanamo Bay?" Becky asked.

"You're in a lot of trouble, Miss Glidden. That's where you are. A lot of trouble and on borrowed time," Walker said, exiting the room.

He felt great about his performance and the way everything was shaping up. He knew he had pushed the right buttons on her and that she was riled up and ready to flee, most likely to her ex-boyfriend's lab to grab enough of the serum to be able to start again in some other time and place, before destroying the rest. Walker knew she would never get past the door of the lab before being brought down by hundreds of armed guards.

He radioed to a man in the facilities office and gave him the go-ahead for the blackout in a little over an hour. This would give Becky the chance to escape, grab Peter and go on her merry way.

Walker felt like a genius and smiled as he gave himself a mental pat on the back.

A little over an hour later, the lights went out. Sirens started sounding and a computerized female voice began making announcements throughout the facility.

"Power grid error," she stated flatly. "Code one."

She repeated this message for several minutes.

Becky felt her restraints change. They were no longer rigid with an electrical current flowing through them. They were still too tight for her to take them off, but she thought she could blink her way out of this room and into Peter's if she concentrated hard enough. She put the image of Peter, curled up in a fetal position on the floor of his cell, into her mind and sent herself there.

For a brief moment she thought she was doomed and that the restraints had left her mind weakened. Part of her thought that she might be in some trouble, because the power would soon come back on and she would be stuck here again. Just when she was ready to quit, exhausted from her attempt to escape, it worked. She was standing in Peter's darkened cell, the robot voice warning security staff that the power grid was down, that all cell doors were no longer functional, that security had been breached.

Becky got down to her knees to grab Peter.

"Come on, Peter. We've got to go," she said, trying to cajole him into standing up.

Peter, barely conscious, looked into her eyes through a swollen face. Becky's heart caught in her throat and the level of emotion she felt for her captive surprised her. She had felt that there was a connection between them, but she did not think it would be this strong so soon, especially when he still likely felt that he was being held against his will.

She lifted him to his feet and embraced him.

"I'm here, baby," she whispered. "No one will hurt you anymore. We're getting the hell out of here."

She focused on a place that she had kept secret and hidden from Peter. She had gone there many times since she had abducted him and even though the trips had been brief - 10 minutes here, 20 minutes there - it gave her a sense of peace and tranquility that she found absolutely necessary to keep her homicidal tendencies at bay.

It was a small cottage in 18th century Bavaria located deep in the Black Forest and nestled in a cove of trees. The cottage was built near the bank of a swiftly moving river and Becky would often come here in the summer time to lazily sweep her feet in the water.

She had stumbled upon the house while cross-country skiing there on an exchange trip in high school and was struck by it's simplicity and functionality. It seemed like a terrific place to live and Becky would often daydream about going there and being away from the pain that came from living with a murdering daddy in prison and a bitter and tired mother who kept her daughter at a distance by throwing money at her. When

Becky got the power to time travel, she wanted to see it when it was originally built and it was just as fantastic as she thought it would be.

The only problem was that it was occupied by an older man living on his own. She saw that there was a grave, most likely belonging to his late wife, a few hundred yards away in a patch of wildflowers, and she helped the man along on his journey to meet her in the afterlife.

And then it was hers. Her perfect little refuge from a world going increasingly mad. She was glad Peter was with her here. She could envision them spending the rest of their lives here - or at least using it as a base of operations.

Becky helped Peter into the cottage and placed him on the bed. She went outside to fetch a pail of water and returned to wipe the blood from his face and to offer him the crisp, clear water to drink.

Peter slept for most of the day and through the night and Becky sat in a sturdy wooden chair by a small table and plotted her next move.

Those people who had abducted her and Peter would have to pay, that was for sure, but something else seemed out of place. Her mind, which had been running on pure adrenaline, felt like it could merely dance on a number of topics instead of going into any of them in depth. The same thing happened when she tried to go to sleep next to Peter that night, so she got up and walked out to the river once more to dip her feet in the incredibly frigid water. It numbed her toes and she would remove them for several minutes at a time to warm them back up again before submerging them once more.

Peter was better the next day and Becky gently asked him questions about what happened at the place their captors had taken them to.

"I don't know," Peter said. "They know about your ability to time travel and they think I have some power too. They kept trying to get me to tell me about it or show them and when I didn't, they tortured me."

Those bastards, Becky thought. They probably thought Peter had invented the formula that triggered the on-set of Becky's power.

"Did they ask you about a formula?" Becky asked.

Peter had to tread carefully here. He needed to make Becky believe that they already knew the location and were going to head there.

"They asked me when I first made it," Peter said. "I don't know when your ex-boyfriend made it and they got really mad when I couldn't tell them."

Becky figured out that the agents, who could obviously time travel themselves, were going to try and get to the formula before she got shot up with it. She and Peter would aim for a few days earlier and beat them to the punch.

Truthfully, Becky had known this day was coming. She knew that her actions were messing with what sci-fi geeks would call the space-time continuum. If time is linear, and as far as she knew it was, her actions were making time split off into very strange tangents. The fact that she couldn't leave well enough alone and kept killing people made things worse.

Killing Cassidy Samuels did keep her father out of prison and it did keep him in her life, but who knew what Cassidy would have done with her life. Or her baby, Becky's half-brother. Becky felt a tinge of sadness at the thoughts of lives unfulfilled, but she wouldn't take it back, even though, technically, she could. It may have been extremely selfish, but, as Becky saw it, that was just the nature of humanity. The "I'll worry about you after I get what I want" principle.

The real question was why did Becky keep on killing? She claimed Alice Parker was to throw the cops off, but they had no clue about who the real killer was. Alice's abduction may have actually caused more harm in Salem, because to the feeble minds of the townsfolk, her disappearance could be seen as proof of witchcraft. Dozens more people had likely been executed because of Becky's action. Again, Becky sighed at her lack of control, but she refused to shed a tear over the idiotic pilgrims. The old German man was killed because Becky wanted his house and he was so close to death and so sad and lonely anyway that she saw what she had done as a mercy killing. He had fear in his eyes and struggled against her hands as she strangled him, but she felt that he found peace as the breath left his body. Becky had shut his eyes and said "you're welcome," before burying him.

Becky knew she had a lot more in her. In fact, she was looking forward to slicing and dicing her way through history. She liked feeling powerful and she found it thrilling to watch someone's life ebb away under her hands. With the billions of people who have ever lived, there were plenty of people to quench her ever-increasing bloodlust. Becky had not been a powerful girl when she was younger. She had no control over anything. Now, she had power and people, even though they didn't know it, feared her and respected her. Power and respect, based on fear, made her feel like the God that she had heard all about at church as an impressionable little girl.

They said she, and everyone else, were sinners. Becky, who felt like an orphan in her own home, felt that God was already punishing her, but she couldn't think of what sin she could have possibly committed. After a moderately deep conversation over cheap beer and Pink Floyd songs with some friends in high school, Becky realized that God was just a convenient way to try and keep people in line.

Becky was now way out of line, but there was no God to stop her. She was the closest thing to God and she could punish whoever she wanted to. Although she found it even more fun to be a randomly vengeful deity.

Peter tended to balk at killing people, but she wondered if he was now closer to her side because of the beating he took. She was sure that he would want to take the serum, just to see what power it might trigger in his brain. Would it be time travel or something else, something better? What could be better? Flight? Invisibility? Pyrokinesis? She practically couldn't wait to see what would happen to him, feeling like a kid on Christmas Eve. They would leave when he woke up.

Becky began to poke at him, trying to rouse him.

Chapter 13

There are people that will investigate you
They'll insinuate, intimidate and complicate you
Don't ever wait or hesitate to state the fate that awaits those who
Try to shake or take you
Don't let them break you

"Do Anything You Want To" - Thin Lizzy

Becky and Peter arrived at a small, brick covered house on a bit of a beat down street. The lawn was overgrown and the paint on the window shutters was a cracked and peeling gray shade of white. The other homes on the silent street looked similar and it gave Peter the sense of being in a neighborhood on the wrong side of the tracks. Becky was riding a wave of nostalgia looking at a place she had called home for over three years.

She had been clutching Peter's hands tightly, but now she let them go and started to walk a few steps ahead. Peter's pace was a little slower and more deliberate, but he didn't need to lean on Becky to keep himself up anymore.

He wondered if Becky was going to knock or simply let herself in. She did neither, choosing instead to look at the newspaper on the front porch and check the date. She had aimed them correctly, landing at the house exactly three days before Eric had given her the serum. Peter tried to crane his eyes at the headlines and the general layout of the paper. Once a newspaper gets in your blood, it is hard to not look at every paper and compare yours to it. He had to admit, and his short time back at 'The Clarion" had proved it, he was a newspaperman. But what if he never went back to work, he wondered, then what kind of a man would he be?

Today, he would find out what he had in his heart and his guts. The adrenaline and steely resolve put a bit of a jump in Peter's step, sharpening his focus and readying himself for the arrival of the agents, who were sure to come at any minute now that he and Becky were at the lab site.

"Let's walk around back and see where Eric and I are," Becky said. Peter nodded and started to follow her. The lawn was filled with weeds, as well as empty beer cans, broken beer bottles and what Peter thought were BBs.

"Eric and I used to shoot at beer bottles with his BB gun," Becky admitted sheepishly. "It was a good way to relieve stress for him and, well, we were typically drunk or high."

Peter knew the types of stupid things that people could do when they were fucked up from personal experience. He was just glad he wouldn't be the next person to mow this lawn. That person had a tetanus shot and possibly stitches in his or her future.

Becky squatted down and peered into a grimy window looking in on a room in the basement.

"This is Eric's lab," Becky explained. "It looks like he's still asleep upstairs, so we should be safe to go in."

They went back to the front door and Becky pulled the spare key from beneath a house plant. She unlocked the door and put the key back in its hiding spot.

As criminal as some of Peter's activities had been in the past, he had never actively participated in breaking and entering. Technically, he still wasn't, as Becky was a resident of this place. It felt sneaky though and it was obvious that Becky was trying to avoid a confrontation with her (ex) boyfriend and/or herself, if possible. She even gave Peter the "shush" finger and started to walk softly across the living room to the basement door.

They reached the steps and Becky went down first, taking each wooden plank step at a time, hesitating at every step to make sure it hadn't made enough noise to wake anybody up.

Peter found it strange to see Becky so scared by the possibility of getting caught. She was as strong a woman as he had ever met, she had even killed people without remorse, and yet she walked in the house as if she were a school girl coming in past curfew and hoping to not get caught. Her trepidation spread to him, keying up his nerves so much that every sore muscle in his body tensed waiting for someone to jump out at them. She had spoken very little about her boyfriend, Eric, but he could see that she was terrified of him.

Peter also reminded himself that a past, time-travel less, Becky was in the house, too. He was sure Becky didn't want to freak herself out and alter her future. Messing with the timeline for the rest of the world was one thing, but Peter would bet dollars to donuts that Becky didn't want to change much of anything about her current path.

After what seemed like hundreds of tiny, quiet steps, both of them had reached the floor of Eric's basement lab. It did not resemble the image that Peter had in his head of a mad scientist's lab. It was not sterile or well organized. It's smell was less of chemicals and more of something like dead animal and something musty and dank. It reminded Peter of the meth labs that he had seen people build out in the woods behind their house. Yes, there were chemicals cooking in glass and plastic vessels, but it would not be confused with a laboratory or Dr. Frankenstein's layer for that matter.

Meth had fortunately been a very brief experiment for Peter. He obviously had an addictive personality and how he dodged a bullet that had plugged so many of his friends back home was beyond him. Peter had always jokingly chalked it up to liking sleep too much to do meth and yet, in those last few weeks before getting his job at The Clarion back, he had been taking those little white energy pills. Legal meth in a way, but it didn't compare to the crank that the speed freaks in Cabot smoked, drank, shot up or snorted. The pills weren't good for him, but they would tweak him for a little while and he could put his hands on them without visiting his old haunts and the skeevy people who haunted them.

Eric and Becky's house definitely had the "drug den" feeling and Peter knew, if he was given a chance, he could unearth a lot of their dirty little secrets.

"Come take a look at this, Peter," Becky whispered. She stood before a large, triangular shaped beaker filled with a pink mixture.

"Here she is," Becky proclaimed, holding it up triumphantly. "Trigger Juice."

The name left a little something to be desired as far as Peter was concerned.

"I think you should take a shot," Becky said.

Peter shook his head.

"I don't think so, Becky. I'm not sure what it would do to me."

"It won't do anything bad, silly," Becky said, trying to sound reassuring.

"You know that from what, two tests on humans?" Peter asked, watching Becky's eyes sharpen as she began to glare at him. He felt she was starting to question his loyalty to her and her cause. Beads of sweat started to form on his forehead as he began to silently pray for the cavalry to arrive.

"Aren't you with me?" Becky said, more than a little loud. "Those bastards would have killed you for a chance to get this. You could have a power of the gods."

Peter tried to quiet her, leading by example, shushing her and answering in a whisper.

"I'm just scared, Becky," he said. "This is all happening so fast. The other day I'm just an unemployed recovering addict and now I'm a time-traveling accomplice to a fugitive murderer."

Becky could see how Peter thought she was being hard on him. She took hold of one of his hands with both of hers.

"I'm sorry, baby, but things are crazy for me, too," she said. "These people are trying to take everything away from me and I can't let that happen. You can help me, especially if I give you this shot and it gives you a cool power like mine. Don't you want to be powerful?"

Oh God, yes, Peter thought. He desperately wanted to be powerful. Powerful enough to stop her, powerful enough to stay clean, powerful enough to get all the things in life that he wanted. Unless the agents came soon, Peter would let her give him the shot and let the chips fall where they may.

"I'll do it, Becky," he said. "For you."

Becky looked downright giddy as Peter rolled up his sleeve and grabbed the side of Eric's sawdust covered workbench. She filled a small syringe with the liquid and tapped out any air bubbles that may be hiding. Peter cringed. His eyes were shut and he was grimacing, anticipating a punch and then the plunge.

"Have you ever given someone a shot before?" Peter asked.

Becky looped an elastic band around Peter's arm, found a vein and slid it in gently.

"Of course I have, silly." she said cheerily, untying the elastic band and cleaning up the area.

They were needle drug users, Peter thought, and instantly wanted to shower and get an AIDS test. Straight-edged people would see Peter's animosity to needle drug users as hypocrisy, considering the fact that he had done his share of drugs back in the day, but he was not being hypocritical. Everyone has their limits and many of the people he knew drew the line at powders and needles.

He rubbed the spot on his arm where Becky had given him the shot and looked around the room. He saw a hulking figure in the shadows and was instantly thrown to the wall by an unseen force.

"Who the hell are you, buddy?" a voice bellowed. Becky turned around shocked, palming the syringe and trying to see if she could get them out of this without a lot of damage.

"Hey baby,-" she started, but was quickly interrupted by a backhand from Eric.

"Hey baby?" he questioned. "Hey baby? You broke my one rule, honey. This lab is mine. No one is allowed in here, not even you! And now you brought some old guy in here? Are you fucking this dude?" Eric asked, breathing heavily with his anger and still holding Peter to the wall with the will of his mind. Peter was a little struck by Eric's statement of him being old. He may not look like he was in his early 30s, but he was still only 32 years old. He guessed the violence done to him by the agency didn't help matters.

"No, I am not fucking him, Eric," Becky said adamantly. "This is our neighbor, Henry. I found him beaten up on the street this morning and he needed some help. I was looking for your first aid kit."

Eric let Peter slide to the floor.

"The first aid kit isn't in my secret, private lab," Eric said, walking slowly up to Becky and speaking quietly. "You know he shouldn't be down here and neither should you."

"I was just trying to be nice," Becky said softly, visibly afraid of her former boyfriend and this situation spiraling disastrously out of control.

Eric turned his attention to Peter, who was still sitting on the floor, the chemicals racing through his blood stream and sounding alarms at all the nerve endings it passed. Peter felt his body was screaming on the inside, like the noisiest parts of a carnival - all bells, whistles, bright, flashing lights and shouting.

"So, Henry, is it? You live up the street?" Eric asked. Oh shit, Peter thought, this is a trap.

Peter hesitantly nodded.

"What number?" Eric asked. Damn it, Peter thought. He tried to remember the address number of this house and couldn't place it. He had to guess and if he guessed wrong, he was going to get another beating and this one might not stop until he was dead. Where were those people from the agency and what were they waiting for, he wondered.

"112," Peter said, trying to obscure the number in a mumble at the end.

"112, did you say? You know Teddy Watson and his family?"

I'm dead, Peter thought. He desperately wanted to look at Becky for help, but that would ignite the situation even more.

"No. I don't know them," Peter said.

"Huh, that's strange," said Eric with a hint of surprise. "I thought you'd know the people that live in the same house as you." Eric seemed to chuckle a bit at catching Peter in a lie and Peter broke out in a sheepish grin that disappeared when he was thrown up against the wall again. Eric pulled a flat head screwdriver off of the work bench and held it to his throat.

"Who are you really, Mr. Henry whoever you are?" Eric asked. Peter stared down at Eric and saw his sweaty and dandruff flaked hair. He could smell the acrid aroma of alcohol coming out of Eric's sweaty pores and the fetid breath of sleep mixed with cigarettes.

Peter tried to focus on flashing his way out of here. It would blow his cover and prevent the agency from capturing Becky and getting a sample of the serum, but he would be safe. Unfortunately, Eric started to hit him in the gut, the screwdriver tightly rolled in his fist. Peter could barely find his breath, much less focus on traveling to a safer time and place.

Becky begged Eric to stop, trying to coax the hulking mass of her ex-boyfriend off of Peter, but he shoved her backwards and she crashed into a workbench, toppling over empty bottles, test tubes, bunsen burners and loose cables.

The rough wood of the work bench scraped her back pretty good, opening up a bit of a bloody wound. As she touched the marks with her fingers and looked at the red liquid pooled on them, she became incensed. She would kill Eric, again, only this time it would be a few days sooner, and she would have to be sure to give her past self, the one who was either still sleeping (not likely) or out running chores (more likely), the shot so that this current future of hers would still be possible. Becky patted herself on the back for having that type of foresight. She filled another syringe quickly, while Eric roughed up Peter, shouting for answers and not getting any.

Peter, who was still nursing some bumps and bruises from his scrape with the agency, was once again in a crippling amount of pain. He also thought that there was a very real possibility of sustaining some serious internal bleeding, if it hadn't started already, because of Eric's punches to where Peter figured his spleen was. As he reeled from the onslaught of punches and kept trying to swing and kick his way to some form of protection, a primal part of his brain kicked in and, without realizing it, triggered the part of his brain that the shot enabled.

Peter's focus on Eric was intense and in the blink of an eye, Eric started to stagger back, appearing to be beaten by an unseen force. It took Peter a second to realize that he was controlling the invisible force that was kicking and punching Eric across the room. He thought about trying to hurl Eric to the wall and hold him there and it happened. It appeared as if Peter now shared the same power as Eric. He had to admit it was coming in very handy right now.

With Eric pinned to the wall, Peter had time to ponder his new found talent. When he had thought about punching, it had appeared that Eric had been punched. What would happen if Peter thought about cutting Eric, would he need a blade? Would he need a gun to shoot him? How much of this had Eric already figured out, Peter wondered, also debating just how he was going to get out of this situation without killing the very angry scientist. If Peter didn't at least knock him out, Eric would undoubtedly get the upper hand and this fight could rage on for hours.

Peter decided to choke Eric just enough to knock him out. He focused his stare on Eric's eyes, looking into them for signs of unconsciousness setting in. When his eyes closed, Peter allowed him to fall to the ground.

He was triumphant and he had to admit it felt good. Peter had never won a fight before and the last time he had actually been in one was the summer before seventh grade. So what if he didn't use brute strength to win this fight. He had defeated a powerful foe and it felt great. He stood looking down at his vanquished opponent and jumped back as a blade swooped down and chopped at Eric's neck. Peter let out a small yelp and turned to see Becky slamming down an axe once again, this time finishing the job and beheading Eric.

"What the fuck!" Peter screamed. "Why did you do that?"

"I had to Peter," Becky said. "I did it before and I'll do it a thousand more times if I have to."

She dragged the headless corpse of her ex-boyfriend to a corner of the basement and covered him with a large blanket. Peter gawped at her, unable to get used to the violence. He had an urge to hit her, just to knock her down and try to get some sense into her. He gritted his teeth but couldn't suppress the urge anymore and Becky fell forward, letting out an "oof" as Peter's "force" belted her forwards.

"Don't hit me, Peter," Becky warned, wagging a finger at Peter's face. "You may feel all-powerful right now, but I can still take you out."

She shifted Eric's head towards the blanket with her feet, trying to avoid getting blood and other forms of assorted goop on her shoes.

"Eric tried to get all high and mighty on me and push me around, once he didn't have to use his hands anymore, but I refused to take that kind of shit," Becky said. "He was man enough to treat me right when he wasn't a supernatural super being, he didn't have to become a supernatural asshole, but he did and he paid the price."

Peter had been put in his place.

"I'm sorry," he said.

"I know!" she yelled. "Follow me," Becky ascended the stairs, this time not trying to be quiet at all. If there was anybody else home, namely herself, she didn't care if past Becky ran, walked or crawled. She was going to get the shot that was meant for her, the one that would change her life forever.

Becky went through the house like a member of a SWAT team, kicking doors open and shouting, trying to scare her prey into an involuntary scream or spasm.

"It's O.k., Becky, come on out," she called. "The bad man is gone."

The bad woman, however, was an entirely different story, Peter thought to himself.

After scanning the bedroom, bathroom and gym/office, Becky turned to Peter, putting a finger to her lips.

"I guess I must be out grocery shopping or something," she said. "Let's come back later."

Becky took a few steps in the hardwood floored hallway and then stood in one place slapping her feet down to sound like she was continuing to walk out. She gestured for Peter to do the same. They stood frozen in the hallway, watching for the past version of Becky to try to escape the room. Within minutes they were rewarded and present Becky sprinted after the scared young woman and pounced on her in the bedroom.

Past Becky screamed. It was quite possibly the most awful sound that Peter had ever heard. It was primal and filled with fear and dread. He imagined that past Becky couldn't wrap her mind around seeing herself on top of her, holding a loaded syringe in front of her face.

The screaming did not last long because present Becky cold-cocked her younger self and knocked her out.

"That was really weird," Becky said. "Give me your belt," she directed Peter. He withdrew the belt from the loops of his jeans and handed it to her. She wrapped it around the unconscious girl's arm, found a vein and plunged the serum into her bloodstream.

"Let's get out of here," Peter suggested. "If we're gone by the time she wakes up, maybe she'll think it was all just a bad dream."

It was a stab in the dark, but it was worth a try. A frightened Becky who never found out she could time travel wouldn't cause all of the problems that she had this time around. The world could be spared from her psychotic rage and menace.

"No," Becky said flatly. "She needs to know what she is capable of."

Before Peter could answer back, a terrible crashing sound came from the front door. A SWAT team splintered the door into shards and a half dozen armed men in black charged in.

"Friends of yours?" Peter asked Becky.

"I was going to ask you the same thing," she replied, reaching for her younger self's hands and closing her eyes.

"What about me?" Peter asked. "You're just going to leave me here?"

"I'll come back for you," she said, with a hint of mistrust and malice. "Besides, I don't think these people want you dead. Do they, Peter?"

A gunshot went off and Peter saw it nick Becky's shoulder, ripping a piece off her shirt and causing a small gush of blood to jump into the air. Becky screamed briefly before trying to submerge it and leave the scene.

"Becky, help me," Peter cried out. "I don't want to be stuck in some future prison." He was trying anything to delay her from jumping out of this time and into some other time and place. She wasn't listening, just trying to meditate in seconds flat and get the hell out of Dodge.

"Find your shot and take it, but nothing fatal," a voice called out. It was Walker, standing far behind the fray. "I want her alive. Both of them."

Several more gunshots were heard and Becky once again focused on escaping. This time she was successful.

Chapter 14

And I Sleep, and I dream of the person I might have been, and I'll be free again
And I Speak, like someone who's been to the highest peaks, and back again
And I Swear, that my grass is greener than anyone's, until I believe again
Then I Wake, and the dream fades away and I face the day and I realize
That there's got to be some hero in me

"Hero in Me" - Jeffrey Gaines

"What took you so long?" Peter yelled at Walker, standing in front of the older man's face and pointing his index finger. "This whole thing got completely screwed up."

"Did it?" Walker asked with a smile. He walked over to the refrigerator and opened the door, grabbing a beer and offering it to Peter. Peter shook his head and Walker twisted the cap off and took a big pull. "They just don't make beer like this in the future."

"Yes, it all got screwed up," Peter stated. "You didn't stop the psycho from gaining the power of time travel or prevent the girl from learning about her power. You got me shot up with the chemical cocktail and the inventor got his friggin' head cut off."

"We just see things differently, Peter," Walker said, sitting on a futon folded up to serve as a couch. "We want Becky to have the power, we would just rather she use it wisely and not to murder thousands of people."

Walker took another pull of beer and sighed contentedly.

"You have an awesome new power and that is not a bad thing, is it? And so what if that guy lost his head? He was an asshole. Worse than that, he was a dangerous asshole. If he lives, he causes almost as many problems as Becky does. Let's just be glad, she destroyed him, because together they could destroy the world."

Peter shook his head and paced around the tiny living room space.

"Hey, big guy, relax," Walker said. "She didn't escape with the serum, we've secured it and will take it back to our lab, analyze it and put in the research and effort that Eric the headless should have. Who knows what kind of things we'll be able to accomplish. That was a huge coup, believe me."

Peter nodded briefly, pursing his lips a bit in doubt.

"But she got away," Peter said.

"She didn't go far," Walker stated. "You weren't the only one who got a chip implanted while under our care."

Peter was incredulous.

"Then what did you need me for?" he yelled.

Walker stood up and approached Peter, placing a hand on his shoulder.

"Hey now, don't be like that," he said. "We weren't using you as bait or anything like that. Everything we had hoped would happen, happened. You are now, quite possibly, the only person who can stop her, right all of her wrongs and convince her to fight on the side of right."

Peter was confused. He had been under a lot of stress lately and sometimes his brain felt fried and a little muddled. He struggled with putting their plan together and why they had him in the center of all of them.

"You may not have asked to be brought into all this, Peter, but you have been and I, for one, am glad," Walker said. "You're a superhero now and you're a perfect fit, if I do say so myself."

Peter dropped to the futon and sat stunned at Walker's last statement. He had rarely ever been considered a good guy, much less a hero, and yet, here he stood, on the precipice of greatness.

"You like that idea, I see," Walker said. "Good. The first step in being great is having good self-esteem. You aren't that miserable piece of crap you once were, Peter. You knew you could be better and you've been working towards a moment of greatness like this for a long time now."

Peter was still too stunned to talk. He had come a long way since the days of public intoxication and discharging weapons into parking lots. He expected to live a quiet existence of penitence, maybe finding someone who knew nothing of his sordid past and could love him for the person he had become, but he never thought he would be involved in anything where the fate of the world hung in the balance. It was daunting, but he felt he had always worked well under pressure.

"O.K., Peter, we have to get out of here," Walker said. "Becky is going to want to put past Becky back here, so that she can become future Becky - aww, you know what I mean. Anyway, let's skedaddle and get you up to speed on what you can do and what we expect you to do."

Peter stood up and Walker grabbed his hands.

"Take us to your apartment, back in your time, November 2007," Walker said. Peter thought of his messy bedroom in his rather spartan apartment and kept silently repeating the words 'back home' in his mind and soon enough, they were there.

Peter was thrilled to be back at his apartment, as old and dingy as it was. It may have been in a questionable neighborhood and it may have smelled like vegetable soup, but it was home.

He wandered around the place as if to make sure everything was still there. His kitchen still had its table with sticky rings made from his coffee mugs and his bedroom still had its broken shade over the window, its lampshade-less lamp and its charcoal gray comforter piled loosely on one side of the bed. His shower curtain hung, just barely, from two rusty metal rings.

"Wow, so this is your home, huh?" Walker asked. "Be it ever so humble."

"Hey, up until recently, I've been out of work," Peter said, chuckling. Even the sorry state of affairs couldn't diminish the fact that he was home, safe and being counted on to protect the world. He felt healthy and powerful and it brought a smile to his face.

"Well, believe me, Peter, help us out of this current crisis, and you'll never have to worry about money again," said Walker. "We'll be able to take care of you, no matter wherever or whenever you choose to live and work out of."

Peter was giddy at this news, as well. His feelings of doubt about fighting and defeating Becky were gone. He found himself now believing that he could win, because all he would have to do is convince her to help him fix the past, use her power for good and stay with and love him. He guessed in a way that he would be asking her to marry him and that made him happy too, because she knew all about him and his less than perfect past and loved him anyway.

Walker snapped Peter out of his euphoria.

"I'm glad that makes you happy, Peter, but you've got a lot of work to do," he said. "First, go get yourself cleaned up."

Peter glanced down at his clothes and realized that he was wearing the same clothes he had been wearing since going to Woodstock and they were covered in dirt and a lot of what Peter figured to be blood. He touched his face and realized that it was swollen, sore and crusted with blood.

"I'm going to go take a shower," Peter said.

"Good idea," Walker stated, then asking, "Do you have any beer?"

Peter tried to avoid looking in the mirror after he started the shower, but it was a force of habit. His face was bruised pretty good and his lip was swollen and split. Peter also had his first black eye in over 20 years. The only other time he got a black eye was when he caught a football with his face in gym class. If half the sixth grade hadn't seen it happen, it may have enhanced his reputation.

By all rights, Peter should have been dead on his feet, but he found himself eager to wash the grime off his body and get to work. He really wanted to test the limits of his power, so he scrubbed, lathered and rinsed as fast as he could. Once out and wrapped in a towel, he applied some Ben Gay to the sorest of his sore muscles and changed into a new pair of jeans and his favorite t-shirt, a Nirvana shirt that featured a map of Dante's nine circles of Hell. He felt like a new man because he was a new man.

Peter entered the living room looking for Walker and didn't see the staff directed toward his legs that swept him from his feet.

"Oww," Peter yelled, looking up and seeing Walker prepared to swing down the staff with full force. "What the hell?"

"We're not talking, Peter," Walker said. "We're training. Just trust your instincts and react."

Walker brought the staff down quickly and hit Peter in his gut, which was still sticky and warm from the patch of Ben Gay that was resting there, trying to soothe Peter's muscles. When Walker immediately prepared to swing again, Peter thought about knocking the staff loose and saw it fly and crash into the wall in the kitchen.

"Good," Walker said, spinning on his right leg and kicking out with his right. His right foot connected with Peter's chest as Peter was trying to raise himself up. Knocked back to the floor, Peter spun and tried to kick Walker's leg out from under him. When it didn't work, Peter envisioned lifting Walker by his foot and tossing him up at the ceiling. Walker, like any man, was unprepared to have his back up against a ceiling and was doubly unprepared to fall quickly back down face first to the floor.

Peter cringed and quickly stepped to him, offering his hand.

"No," Walker said. "I'm fine. Don't worry about me."

"I guess I don't know my own strength," Peter said.

"You will," Walker said, smiling. "It will all come together for you and sooner rather than later."

Peter had no reason to trust Walker more now than he had a few days earlier, but he did. It appeared that everything Walker said would happen did happen and when things didn't go as Peter had thought they would, there seemed to be a reasonable explanation.

The two men were taking a bit of a breather as Walker got to his feet.

"One thing I want you to start doing Peter is becoming more aware of your surroundings," Walker said. "There are a lot of weapons around here. Some of them might only be good as distractions, but others could do some damage."

Peter glanced around his apartment and saw the distractions that Walker was talking about. There were curtains, blankets and pillows and Peter found he could levitate them with just a thought in their direction. They could slow down a charging enemy, but Peter didn't see anything that could do damage.

"Where are these dangerous items I could use?" Peter asked.

"Break the glass in the windows or turn the gas on your stove on and light a match," Walker said. "And I assume there are knives in this pigsty somewhere, right?"

Peter nodded.

"Find one," Walker directed and Peter started to move towards the kitchen. "No, stay here and have one come to you."

Peter thought about his kitchen and the silverware drawer to the left of the sink. He pictured it opening and he thought about levitating a steak knife and directing it out of the kitchen, around the corner into the hallway and into his hand, handle towards his palm.

"Very good," Walker said. "You really got the hang of this very quickly. That's good."

Peter practiced moving items with his mind at a variety of speeds. He concluded with a spectacular finale involving several knives spinning next to each other in opposite directions. It would have been very painful for anyone who got in its path.

"I think I'm getting really good at this," Peter said after what had amounted to a few hours of training.

Walker smiled and shook his head.

"I'm glad you feel good, Peter, but you shouldn't get overly confident," Walker said, grabbing another beer out of the refrigerator. "I wish we could give you months and years of training, but we just don't have that kind of time."

"Where is she?" Peter asked, wondering if he was going to be thrown into the fire in a matter of minutes. As comfortable as he was starting to feel with his powers, he wasn't exactly excited to put them to use in a life or death situation so soon.

Walker looked at a small screen attached to his very modern looking version of a cell phone. He looked relieved.

"She is still in her little sanctuary in Germany, but we expect that she'll be on the move soon," he said.

"Shouldn't I go there?" Peter asked. "There's a much smaller chance of any collateral damage occurring."

"No, Peter, we're sending you someplace else," Walker said.

"Where?" Peter asked.

"Right here, Halloween 2007."

Halloween, Peter remembered, was the day that Becky murdered Cassidy Samuels. Peter had established a semblance of security for Cassidy by having Detective Leonard post police officers along her path that night, but there was always a part of him who assumed that Becky would be coming back to this night to make sure she was able to finish the job. He just didn't think he would have to be the one to stop her.

"I can convince her not to kill Cassidy," Peter said, but Walker shook his head and looked at the floor as Peter continued. "Let me go to her right now and I can lay it all out for her."

"Look, I won't lie to you. We'd love to have Becky as an ally, but we're not sure that is very likely," Walker said, pausing and sitting down on the sofa. "I'm afraid I haven't been completely honest with you, Peter."

"Well, start, please," Peter said more than a little angrily.

"We need you to save Cassidy Samuels - more specifically, we need you to save her unborn baby," Walker said. "He is the key to a peaceful and safe planet. Hell, he is the key to a peaceful and safe galaxy, if you want to get technical about it."

"O.K., so why don't I just go and boost her from right after she got pregnant and go put her somewhere safe?" Peter asked, knowing that Walker's answer wouldn't satisfy him.

"Because, if we really want a safe and peaceful world and galaxy, we need to get rid of Becky."

"But I could talk to her, you said -" Peter offered

"No, Peter. You don't understand," Walker said rubbing his face with his hands, knowing his explanation would probably be confusing. "The Becky who just got the trigger serum is with the Becky you know, learning all about her power and being programmed to go to Halloween 2007 and kill Cassidy Samuels, the girl that destroyed her family and made her the drug addicted cretin she currently is. That Becky doesn't know who you are and doesn't care what you say. She will be set loose on Cassidy tonight and, if she isn't stopped, she will forever alter the universe."

Peter turned his back on Walker. He had been lied to and he was angry.

"You said -" he started, but Walker put up his hand to stop him.

"Look, Peter, it may not be right, but I said everything I could to get you where you are right now," Walker stated solemnly. He stood up and started pacing the room. "You have the power to time travel, you have the power of telekinesis, you know where Becky goes tonight and you know the streets of the city like the back of your hand if she deviates from the path. There isn't anybody more suited to stopping this murder from happening and saving the world."

Peter said nothing in response.

"I've said all there is to say," Walker said. "Once you go to Halloween 2007, it will begin. It all starts with you now."

Peter nodded.

"One more thing," Walker said, almost apologetically. "It would be better if you didn't run in to yourself. It could really screw up everything that has already happened."

Peter sighed. He paused for a few seconds, expecting there to be at least two or three more things, but when Walker simply looked at him, expecting him to make his move, Peter flashed out of the room.

Chapter 15

Head full of tricks and treats
It leads me thru the nighttime streets
Black cats and falling trees
Under ladders always walking
Salt shaker spills just throw it over your shoulder, babe
I've got a bad idea again, I've got a Halloweenhead

"Halloweenhead" Ryan Adams

Peter had focused on the gazebo and fountain at the center of town. On Halloween day, the local school children marched downtown in their costumes and placed their decorated pumpkins on the paths and sidewalks and at night they returned with their parents and placed lit candles inside.

He looked up at the clock on the old courthouse and saw that it was 3 p.m. School would be letting out soon and Peter wanted to get Cassidy Samuels in his sights.

The only problem was he didn't know what she looked like. He decided to go over to the school anyway, hoping that a brilliant idea or stroke of luck would come his way on the walk. And then he remembered that her face would be on the front of the newspaper in three days, so he stopped at a newspaper box in front of the Buffalo Bill, a roast beef restaurant that Peter had frequented, and thought about jumping to this same spot three days in the future. It worked like a charm and Peter grabbed a copy of the paper and went back to Halloween day, paper in tow.

She was beautiful, Peter thought. Not like a super-model or some of these pageant girls, but pure and happy. In her picture, that is. Cassidy Samuels, a high school junior sleeping with and impregnated by a teacher, obviously had her demons. Yet, the darkness wasn't evident in her school picture. She was looking past the photographer and, Peter thought, past Cabot. That was a thought that was enough to brighten the eyes and smiles of all of the teens in town. As someone who ended up staying in the town he grew up in, Peter knew that most of the kids left town after graduation and rarely came back. He could see in Cassidy's eyes that she was one who, at least in her sophomore year photograph, had her eyes on a prize that was far, far away from Cabot. Of course, she probably hadn't met her "boyfriend" then and she wasn't carrying around a growing secret then either.

Peter hadn't thought of high school girls in years, but his thoughts turned to the ones he knew in his school days as he walked past Macauley's Pharmacy and rounded the corner to the street that would take him to the high school. Did any of the girls he knew carry on illicit affairs with teachers? Did they get themselves into "delicate situations?" It didn't seem possible to Peter. He had almost convinced himself that they had been too young and too innocent for anything like that to happen, but a flood of memories rushed in.

Memories of raucous parties in the woods, wannabe gangsters pulling knives on kids in the restrooms, drug dogs sniffing lockers in the hallways and a near constant stream of talking and thinking about sex. Teenagers in Cabot may gaze off into the distance, dreaming of their future, but the town laid its traps and many people, like Cassidy Samuels and Peter Miller, got trapped.

Peter crossed the street and stood at the top of the hill leading to the school's parking lot. He didn't want to get too close because he would look very suspicious and a bit imposing to the savvy school children, especially on Halloween. He decided to walk down the street and back, buying himself some time, before sitting on the hill to watch football practice. There was no harm in that and he wouldn't be the only adult watching practice. The Cabot team was a perennial contender for conference titles and this year was no different. Peter wondered if they would win state this year and made a mental note to jump ahead a few weeks after all of this was all over to find out.

Peter started to wonder why he had never truly left the town behind. He had left for college and had worked outside of town for a time, but he always came (crawling) back. He had always claimed to hate this place, but upon further consideration he didn't really believe this was true. He may have hated some of the things that had happened to him here and some of the people he felt were to blame (mainly himself when you got right down to it) but there was a lot to like and it was all fairly evident on this unseasonably warm October afternoon. The trees still had a large number of their vividly colored leaves and the ones that had fallen carpeted the streets and puddled themselves against the curbs. The slight breeze scratched them against the pavement and made them dance and swirl. He had seen them on what had been an invigorating walk, which was another thing he loved - the ability to walk to all the good stuff in town. Sure, some mornings, walking in the bitter cold for a coffee, a donut and the paper, was like its own version of Hell, but on days where the weather wasn't miserable, it was a way to see and stay connected to the community.

He reached the entrance to the school parking lot once again and walked a bit inside to reach the hill overlooking the athletic fields. The football team was on its way to the field, jogging out and holding their helmets. The team had been terrible in Peter's day, but a new system and a slew of new kids populating the school had turned things around. He glanced over at the parking lot and started to search for Cassidy. He focused on her picture in the paper until he could see it in his mind and then he tried to summon her his way.

His eyes suddenly flinched away from brightness, as if he had caught a glimpse of the sun reflecting off of a mirror. When he dared to look back a split second later, he saw her and what could only be described as a golden aura. She was walking out of the door that led to the band and chorus rooms and towards the parking lot. Peter hoped she was not heading to a car, as it would be hard for him to keep up with her, and was rewarded as she waved goodbye to some friends and started walking up the hill.

Peter stood up and brushed the dried grass from the seat of his pants. He started to casually walk towards the parking lot, aiming to be far enough behind her that he wouldn't startle or alarm her, but close enough to still see where she was going. Peter also thought to keep his eyes open to look for another pair of eyes following her. Becky may have told her past self all about Cassidy and her path on Halloween, but she could also be showing her. It would be bad news if the Beckys saw Peter following Cassidy.

Cassidy crossed at a cross walk that led to a housing complex in one direction and up the hill and towards the hospital in the other. She walked into a central courtyard in the complex and crossed through. The complex, Glenloch Woods, was deep. Each building housed four apartments, almost like a double duplex, and Peter had no idea how many there were. He did not want to walk into the complex because he knew that there were thousands of eyes in there on the lookout for anything suspicious. The residents there had a lot to look out for - teenagers who rarely came home at night or who might be dealing to their friends and their siblings, abusive husbands and boyfriends looking for ways to finagle their way back into lives or wallets, people serving subpoenas, police officers serving warrants - someone would notice a man following a young girl.

Luckily, he could stay on the sidewalk and peer into the complex in between the buildings. He would casually glance into the yards and find her as he walked and she walked deeper and deeper into the complex. There was a chance that she just cut through Glenloch Woods to get to the houses on the other side. It was a great short cut. As she went deeper, Peter decided that it must be what she was doing. He started to jog up the street and cut through the parking lot behind the middle school at the top of the road. Once safely through there, he cut back and tried to find the street where Cassidy had walked through.

He did not see her through any of the first few streets and he began to pick up his pace. Had he lost her already, he wondered in a mounting panic. What if the Beckys had seen him trying to keep an eye on her and grabbed her just when she was out of his sight? He was back to jogging again and desperately looking for her.

"Are you O.K., mister?" a girl's voice asked. Peter jumped a bit and turned around. It was her. He broke out in a smile.

"I'm fine," he said, reigning in the smile so as not to look like a weirdo.

"Are you looking for someone?" Cassidy asked, appearing concerned.

"My dog," Peter blurted out. "She, uh, ran this way, I think."

"Oh. I'm sorry. Need me to help you look?" she asked, hoping that he would say no. She had heard many stories of kids being abducted like this while she growing up.

"No, that silly thing will show up eventually. She always makes it back home eventually," Peter said. "I'll just keep looking as I make my way home, she's probably already there waiting for me."

Peter started to walk in the direction that Cassidy had been heading.

"You live this way?" she asked.

"Yeah, sort of, Froggy, my dog, likes to go for long walks," Peter said.

"Can I walk with you?" Cassidy asked. Peter smiled and agreed, but inside he hoped he was doing the right thing and that the Beckys weren't watching.

"So, do you go to Cabot High?" Peter asked. Cassidy told him that she did and then filled him in with what classes she liked (very few) and which ones she hated.

"Do you like any of your teachers?" Peter asked and Cassidy hesitated before answering.

"I don't know," she said, which Peter, if he remembered his teen-speak correctly, knew meant that she absolutely did know, she just didn't want to talk about it.

"I didn't like a lot of my teachers at Cabot, either," Peter said.

Cassidy's jaw dropped.

"You went to Cabot?" she asked.

"Yep, class of 1993," he said. "I really hated this one teacher, Mrs. Krutin."

"Ooh, I hate her too," Cassidy said. "She is an evil, old witch."

Peter couldn't believe Krutin was still alive, much less still teaching Chemistry. There had to be thousands and thousands of college graduates each year who were qualified to teach 11th grade Chemistry and teachers like Margaret Krutin clung to their jobs and this mortal coil for what seemed like centuries.

The two walked a few hundred yards in silence, enjoying the day and the sight of bright, pumpkin colored leaves cascading into large piles on the street. Even if he hadn't known about her pregnancy and her affair, he could tell something was bothering her, but, as a stranger with no experience dealing with teenagers outside of his own experiences as a troubled teen, he didn't bother her.

"Going trick or treating tonight," Peter asked. Cassidy rolled her eyes.

"How old do you think I am?" she asked. "I'm going to a big party down by the beach."

Aha, Peter thought. Thanks for the info, kid.

"A costume party?" he asked.

"Duh, it is Halloween," Cassidy said, smiling. "I'm going as Rainbow Brite. It's part of a theme that my friends are doing - old school cartoons."

"I see," Peter said. "Well, if I find my dog, we're heading into Salem for the parade."

"Cool," Cassidy said and Peter knew by her tone that she did not mean it. The annual Halloween parade in Salem, which started well before the adult festivities started, was mainly for people with kids or very basic levels of entertainment.

"This is me," Cassidy said. "It was nice to meet you -" she stopped because she had never learned his name.

"Peter," he said.

"It was nice to meet you, Peter," she said. "I hope you find Froggy."

"Thanks," said Peter, watching Cassidy enter her home. There were several hours before she would be leaving for her Halloween party and a few more after that before she would be brutally murdered by the woman he had dubbed 'The Cabot Butcher.'

Peter decided to work his way back to the movie theater and catch the afternoon show of "Halloween." Frank Vagos, the owner of The Cabot Cinema, owned a pristine print of the film and screened it every year on Halloween. Peter had seen it here every year for almost 20 years now. He thought that sitting in a darkened theater and watching a scary movie would be a good way for him to pass the time. Of the very little he knew Becky Glidden, she seemed like a stickler for tradition and would want to commit the murder as close to the original time as possible.

Peter reached the theater just in time for the 5 p.m. show. He paid his admission to a teenager in a cheesy red vest and bow tie and got a small red ticket. At the concessions counter, Peter ordered a small popcorn, a large Coke and a box of Milk Duds. He inhaled the scent of freshly popped popcorn while he waited and gazed at the classic decor of the theater. It truly was a jewel, especially when you consider that three blocks away was a horribly polluted channel of water, a rusty bridge complete with a village of junkies and homeless underneath, and the scariest bar in town directly across the street from the bridge. Cabot was full of those contrasts.

Peter got his food and went to find a seat in the theater. He nearly jumped out of his skin when he realized that his past self was sitting several rows in front of him.

What am I doing here, Peter thought. I came to the 9 p.m. show, not the 5 p.m.

Peter started to panic. Somehow the timeline had already been tinkered with and he didn't know why or how it was going to effect things.

It was possible it had effected things already, Peter thought. Deciding to try to levitate his Milk Duds box from the cup holder adjacent to him. Everything still worked, so he breathed a sigh of relief, but he couldn't enjoy very much of the film and left before Michael Myers put on the ghost costume and killed the slutty friend.

He entered a tiny cafe across the street, ordered a cup of coffee and read the issue of the Clarion he had picked up earlier that day while he waited for the past version of Peter Miller to leave the theater.

Present Peter would be doing some more reconnaissance today and hopefully it would lead him in the same direction as the Halloween beach party.

Chapter 16

we'll go somewhere
we've never been
time's runnin' out
we'll start again
what's round the bend
I just can't say
let's get away

"Great Jones Street" – Luna

    A little after 6:30 p.m., Peter Miller - the unemployed, powerless one, left the movie theater and walked up the street towards his favorite pizza parlor. He did not go in and order a slice, instead, he rounded the corner and walked down a side street past a closed candy store that he realized he had never been in. He realized this every time he passed it and wondered, every time, why he never went in. He could not go in tonight. He had, as the poet said, miles to go before sleep for one thing, and it was closed for another. He scurried across the street and walked past the library and out towards the commons. Across the street was one of Cabot's several ancient cemeteries and Peter saw a few costumed teens roaming around in the shadows. He motored past the cemetery and crossed the street, heading down to the Jones Street beach.
    Peter Miller - the employed (still?) and super-powered one followed his past self from a little over a block away. He was getting good at tailing people and he was very pleased, but also a little nervous, that past Peter was heading directly towards the beach, where somewhere close by a raging high school party would soon be starting. Present Peter knew something fishy was going on, because he knew what he did on Halloween and it involved taking a double dose of Nyquil, walking to the 9 p.m. showing of "Halloween," taking down three slices of pepperoni pizza and a pitcher of root beer, walking back home, puking into his bathtub and passing out on the fuzzy mat in front of the toilet. The past version of himself looked very focused and determined, much like the present version of himself looked.
    Past Peter had crossed the street to the beach and walked past the worn down and sand blasted playground, up the hill to where a whisper of smoke from a small fire could be seen. Present Peter stayed on the opposite side of the street and kept his eye on the gathering, looking for things to help him guess how many people were there and trying to catch a glimpse of a Rainbow Brite costume. There would be some problems if Cassidy saw past Peter, because she would feel she knew him, having just talked to him hours before, and he would have no idea who she was.
    Everything is such a clusterfuck, Peter thought, promptly trying to regain his cool and figure out a good course of action.
    Once he reached the corner, Present Peter had to decide where to go next. He did not want to be spotted, by either Cassidy or himself, so he crossed the street and walked past the hill, trying to find a place to duck into the woods. He would double back and hide amongst the trees, hoping to see Peter and not Cassidy, not yet. Unfortunately, she was there, drinking something from a red plastic cup and dancing provocatively with a Strawberry Shortcake, a Cabbage Patch Kid and a Care Bear (Grumpy, of course). Out of the corner of her eye, she saw Past Peter and a confused expression crossed her face.

Present Peter seethed at whatever had made the time line screwy, because this poor girl probably thought that another older man was getting ready to proclaim love, lust or a combination of both and try to take advantage of her. He wished he could have prevented this and he swore she would live on after tonight, if only to erase the horrible memories and feelings that must be flooding her mind. Present Peter was a protector.

"What are you doing here?" Cassidy asked, a little louder than she needed to. She was obviously a little tipsy. Several of the partygoers retreated a bit from the fire and got ready to run. They obviously thought this older guy could be a cop of some sort.

Past Peter looked confused.

"Peter, right?" Cassidy asked.

Past Peter nodded.

"How do you know my name?"

"Are you high? You walked me home while you were trying to find your dog," Cassidy snarled.

"I need you to come with me, Cassidy," Past Peter said, his hands out in the open, trying to show that he meant her no harm.

"No fucking way," she said. "I don't even know you. You're a creep."

"Cassidy, you are in grave danger," Past Peter warned. Present Peter thought that he did sound very creepy and he wasn't surprised Cassidy balked at going with him. Good for you, he thought. This guy was obviously on the wrong side of things. Of course, this guy was him, in a sense, but Present Peter would worry about what all of that meant later. Right now, he had to find a way to get in there and get his past self out.

He saw some more partygoers heading towards the fire and decided to try something. He walked down the hill and stopped them. There was a boy painted blue to look like a Smurf, a girl dressed up like Jem and a boy or girl in a Garfield mask.

"I don't think you want to go up there," Peter said to the teens. "It's gonna be raided by the cops any minute."

"How do you know that?" the smurf sneered.

"Because I'm a cop, genius," Peter said, sniffing around their faces. "You three been pre-gaming?"

"No, sir," Jem said in a shaky voice.

"Good," Peter stated officiously. "Hey, Garfield, 20 bucks for the mask."

"Why?" the kid asked in a muffled tone.

"I'm a collector, what do you care?" Peter snapped back.

The two made the exchange and the teens wandered back the way they came.

"Keep your noses clean," Peter shouted out towards them. He placed the mask over his face and walked up the hill.

The scene up there had deteriorated quickly. Cassidy was still yelling at Past Peter and several of the male teens, many of whom were dressed as members of both G.I. Joe and Cobra were circling him and pushing him around.

"I am so sick of skeevy perverts like you," Cassidy yelled. "You ruin everything! We shouldn't always have to look over our shoulders or worry about getting abducted, but we do. People like you have made it so that we grow up in a constant state of fear!"

Cassidy was rallying the troops, as the partygoers, who were previously just fueled on alcohol and weed, were now fueled by rage.

Present Peter ran into the circle, screaming and threw an overhand punch at Peter's face. He then began to pummel Past Peter in the stomach, swearing and screaming incoherently at him. The teens cheered through the first few punches but soon worried that the kid in the Garfield mask was going to kill this guy. A few Cobra soldiers pulled him off Past Peter.

"Now, get out of here!" Cassidy spat at the Peter who was curled up and groaning on the ground.

"I need a drink!" she said and huffily walked back to a cooler near the fire.

Many of the partygoers followed, but Present Peter stayed.

"I just want to see if he's all right," he said to the few kids who were worried about him pummeling the guy on the ground again. "Then I'll make sure he is on his way."

They nodded and walked back to the warmth of the fire and their ill-gotten collection of booze.

Present Peter lifted his mask and looked into Past Peter's eyes, his eyes. It was very unnerving to see the pain he had caused himself and the fear and confusion that lay behind those eyes. Past Peter started to scream, but Present Peter covered his mouth lightly with his hand and spoke in a harsh whisper.

"Be quiet. You don't want them to come back here, do you? "

Past Peter shook his head. Convinced he wouldn't scream, Present Peter removed his hand.

"Who sent you here?" he asked.

"I don't know," Past Peter said. "I got a note telling me to come here and it was attached to this article."

Past Peter sat up and removed the first article about Cassidy Samuels' murder from his pocket.

"The note told me to come here and stop the murder, so I did," Past Peter said. Present Peter breathed a sigh of relief. His past self was a good guy. He didn't know who had sent him here, but the man's intentions were good.

"Are you me?" Past Peter asked.

Present Peter nodded, knowing that everything that had happened to him over the past few weeks could be dissolving because of this encounter. Would the Peter from the past still be in line to get his job back, which led to being abducted, traveling through time and getting the power of telekinesis? Present Peter did not want to lose those things, but he realized that if he stopped the murder of Cassidy Samuels, he would most likely lose those them. It wouldn't stop him from saving her, but it did leave him with a touch of sadness.

"Are you from the future?" Past Peter asked.

"Yeah," Present Peter said.

"How far in the future?"

"Around three weeks," Present Peter said, getting a little irritated. "Look, you have to get out of here. This isn't really a very safe place."

Past Peter rubbed his chin and said "I get that."

Present Peter was a little proud at how well he had done in handing out a beating and how well the past version of himself had taken it.

"What are you supposed to do with her?" Present Peter asked the past version of himself.

"The note says to make sure she reaches the high school safely," Past Peter answered and the blood in Present Peter's veins ran cold. It was clear to him that Becky had sent Past Peter the note and she meant to eliminate both Cassidy and the weaker version of Peter in one fell swoop.

"I'll handle it," he told Past Peter.

"I'm coming with you," Past Peter said and Present Peter growled at his past self's stubbornness.

"I can't have you there, Peter, because if you die, I die. Go somewhere safe. Have Detective Leonard lock you up for the night, " Present Peter said.

"No. I have to do this," Past Peter said. "I need to do something good with my life and if it means saving this girl, then I'm going to do it."

"Yes, you will," Present Peter said. "By which I mean, I will. Look, Peter, I swear, good things are going to happen to you in the next few days and you will do amazing things, but you have to let things happen in their own time. Trust me. Trust yourself."

Past Peter looked at the future version of himself skeptically. He nodded and started to slink back home. Peter felt bad about booting himself home, but he needed to make sure he had a future to go to and that would never come to pass if the past version of himself did something stupid and got himself killed.

Peter readjusted the Garfield mask and raised his arms triumphantly, signaling a victory over the party crasher. The teens cheered and a few offered him quaffs of ale in red plastic cups. He graciously accepted one and dumped out a little bit at a time, while the rest of the party got good and fucked up quickly.

Peter, feeling creepy as hell, started to dance with Cassidy, trying to make sure she would let him walk her home. As she got more and more inebriated, she danced closer and closer to him, until she was practically just embracing him and pulsing her body to the beat of the music. He would casually try to create a little space between them, but she was having none of it. Though he certainly didn't want it to happen, his body was excited by her. He was very uncomfortable and kept trying to think of unpleasant things.

She tried to lift his mask off a few times, but he diverted her attention each time by pointing to another couple getting hot and heavy or the stars.

The party stopped suddenly when a police car flashed its lights on the street. The costumed kids fled in every direction and the cops seemed pleased with this result, choosing to not get out of the car but flash their flashlights on the kids as they scrambled. Peter thought about leading her right over to their car, but decided against it.

If Becky was going to play for keeps, so was he.

Chapter 17

every day it's just another breath
every night another little death
do you scratch and itch when your head feels tight
or wave it away and just stay out all night?

"Saucer-Like" - Sonic Youth

Cassidy agreed to let Peter, or rather Garfield (she still didn't know who he was) walk her home and her friends hadn't stuck around long enough to make sure she made it safely from the party spot. If she died tonight, they would likely blame themselves for scattering so quickly.

Peter knew that the police would be on the main roads, so he took her the back way.

"Do you know where I live, Garfield?" Cassidy asked in a very cute, drunken lilt. Peter said yes.

"I can't hear you behind that mask," she said. "Take it off."

Peter shook his head.

"But I'm not sure I really know who you are," she said, not really worried.

"It's a secret," he said. "I'll show you when I get you home."

This seemed to satisfy her and they walked down the road, past the back of the cemetery and towards the nursery where Peter's family got their Christmas tree every year. This was not a direct route to the high school, but Peter thought the police might drive by this way at some point, so he put Cassidy on the inside of the sidewalk and ushered her towards the first side street he could find that would eventually reconnect with where he wanted to go.

"This isn't where I live, Garfield," Cassidy said.

"I know," Peter said, adding a dramatic pause. "Sorry, I just don't want this night to end."

Cassidy, who was holding Peter's hand, squeezed it a little at this.

"You're a nice guy, Garfield."

"I just want to see you get home safe, is all," Peter said.

"My hero," she cooed and giggled a little.

He hoped he would be her hero when all was said and done, but as the night wore on, his nervousness threatened to make his body go into seizures or choke him with a thick, coppery taste at the back of his throat.

Peter would take Cassidy to the high school, right where Becky wanted her. He knew the unspeakable things Becky had done to Cassidy on the football field, but that was when no one was around.

Things would be different this time.

After crossing a street by one of the many train stops in Cabot, Peter started to walk down a street that would put them closer to the high school. Cassidy recognized that it wasn't her street after they had gone halfway down it already.

"Where are we going?" she asked.

"The high school," Peter said.

"Why?"

Peter couldn't think of anything to say at first. He glanced over at the now very flushed, exhausted and still very drunk Cassidy. She had placed her trust in a guy in a mask and that made Peter a little sad. She had put up a good front after school and at the party, but it was clear to him that she felt she did not have much going for her.

"It's a surprise," he said finally.

"Just so you know, I don't put out on the first date," Cassidy said. Peter smiled behind his mask.

They reached the top of the hill leading to the school's parking lot and Peter did not see anybody on the football field. A police car was heading behind the school, towards the tennis courts and would not come back this way for at least five minutes, if the officer decided to come back this way at all.

Peter plodded down the hill, a sick feeling in his belly, nervously glancing all around him, waiting for one or both of the Becky's to come jumping out at them. By the time they had reached the parking lot and the entrance to the band and chorus room, Cassidy had reached her limit.

"I have to sit down, Garfield," she said, clearly pooped. "I think we just walked two miles."

Peter thought it was closer to three, but nodded.

"Sit down next to me," she said, patting the cold ground next to her.

He reluctantly took a seat but maintained his vigilance, looking out of the corner of the mask's eye holes, watching for the attack that he knew was coming at any minute.

"You're nervous," Cassidy said softly, as if it was the sweetest thing she had ever seen. "Don't be nervous. I won't bite you."

Cassidy once again reached for Peter's mask and he instinctively reached out to try and stop her. She shook her head and he relented. Once the mask was above his lips, she leaned in, eyes closed, and kissed him. He was revolted at himself for instantly knowing it was one of the best kisses in his life. As the kiss went deeper, Peter knew he had to pull back or risk being beheaded by Becky while locking lips with a teenager. He slowly moved away and she opened her eyes and screamed.

"Oh my God," she shrieked, along with a string of profanities and unintelligible syllables and sounds. She tried to get to her feet quickly, but stumbled, before regaining some kind of balance and jogging away towards the courtyard and the entrance to the lunchroom.

"Cassidy, wait," he called. "It's not what you think."

She continued to scream but Peter knew that they weren't close enough to any homes for them to be clearly heard. After all, nobody had heard her when she was being murdered.

Peter followed after her, but she had already rounded the corner to the lunchroom doors. He broke into a run now that she was out of his sight.

"Cassidy, please!" he yelled. "Someone is trying to kill you."

He rounded the corner and saw Becky, holding Cassidy in a choke hold, covering her mouth with a hand and pointing a gun at Peter.

"Someone's trying to kill you, too, lover," she said. Peter instantly thought of grabbing the gun and throwing it. A force ripped it out of her hand and threw it on to the school's roof, where dozens of frisbees and tennis balls had gone to die.

Peter didn't see the Becky behind him though and she swept his legs with a kick and then stepped on his balls after he collapsed to the ground. The two Beckys had apparently been at the school long enough that day to keep the entrance by the lunchroom open, because while Peter was grimacing in pain and blinking back a stinging flood of tears, the two Beckys took Cassidy inside the school.

Peter knew there was not a lot of time. They could easily find a dozen hiding places in the school and, if he didn't get moving quickly, it would be hard for him to find them.

He stood up on unsteady legs and took a number of painful steps. The pain started to subside as the adrenaline kicked in and Peter limped after them into the dark hallways of the school.

"Cassidy," he called. "I won't let them hurt you, but you have to make some noise and let me know where you are."

He heard nothing.

No footsteps, no whispers, nothing.

An empty school is like an empty playground. There is just something very unseemly in certain places when they are devoid of life. A school can be like a living being when it is full of masses of students and faculty going through the machinations of maturing, but empty it is merely a shell.

Peter found it to be very creepy. As if he were crawling around in the belly of a ghost.

He realized he hadn't set foot in this building since his last day of school nearly 15 years earlier. Peter still knew where everything was though. He bet he could even find and open his old locker in the B wing.

Peter gambled and decided to go through the cafeteria. He didn't think they would be in there, necessarily, but it would link him to the field house, the shops and some classrooms.

He walked close to the wall in the cafeteria, skulking and trying to hide in any shadows he could find. Every now and then he would shout, calling for Cassidy or for Becky to give it up. He would then stop in his tracks and listen as hard as he could for any clue of sound. His nerves would be ratcheted up, waiting for any kind of answer, but it did not come.

As he reached the other side of the cafeteria, a Becky came at him with several knives she had apparently borrowed from the kitchen. She slashed wildly at Peter, splitting the air and creating whip like noises. His focus was on dodging the blades, so he could not summon enough focus to hurl her out of his way, but he did throw his arm in the path of the knives. It acted as a bit of a diversion, as Becky sliced away at his arm, tearing through his shirt and skin and opening a good sized wound. He was able to use his other hand though and he slugged her in the face, feeling her nose bend under his fist and a gush of warm blood coat his hand.

Becky reached for her nose and then swung the knives several more times before attempting to run off. Peter gripping his wound, as if he could shut it by holding it together, thought of ripping the knives from her hands. They floated in the air, waiting for his direction, and Becky tried to jump and recapture them. He placed one at her throat and one at her back, forcing her to walk ahead of him.

Perhaps now they could swap hostages.

"Where are they?" Peter asked his captive.

"Go to hell," she snarled.

"I'll kill you and then this will all be over," he warned, forcing the knives to tighten their grips.

"You kill me and she'll kill your girl," Becky warned back.

Peter realized that she was right.

"Let's not end it that way, Becky," he called out, aimlessly walking towards the AV room, which he was sure had undergone massive changes since his days as a student. He wasn't talking to his prisoner and she knew it. He knew that the future Becky, the one he knew, was in control of this whole quagmire. He wanted to talk sense to the sensible one.

"Your Dad won't kill her anymore, " he said. "He won't go to jail. You don't have to do this."

"What if I want to do it?" Prisoner Becky asked. "That little slut needs to pay for fucking my daddy anyway."

Peter found that Prisoner Becky was far crazier and more unhinged than the Becky he had gotten to know. This Becky was strung out and wild. She was like a rabid dog and appeared far more dangerous than the Becky he had traveled with. He had to remind himself that they were the same person.

"Becky, the people who helped me, they can help you, too," Peter said. "They want to help you. They want you to work for them."

Becky, the one not under two knives, answered with a resounding "Fuck them" that echoed throughout the halls of the high school. Peter wasn't sure exactly where it came from, except that it was closer to the classrooms than the gym.

He no longer needed wild Becky as a prisoner, but he couldn't let her loose either. He cracked the door of the A/V room and scanned inside for some materials. Soon, a roll of duct tape and three long extension cords floated out to him. He ripped off several pieces of tape and covered her mouth, bound her with the thick, orange cables and locked her inside the room.

Now there was only one crazy Becky to contend with and he just had to find her.

He walked the floor of the lower level listening for footsteps. What Peter did hear was the door to the outside closing. Becky was still going to try and finish Cassidy off on the 50 yard line of the football field.

Peter grabbed the fire alarm closest to him and pulled the white bar off, making the alarm sound off and hopefully bringing the fire department, police and EMTs to the school as soon as possible. Peter knew his time was limited because Becky knew her time was too.

He ran as fast as he could down to the door to the outside. He was still hobbling a little bit, but he chose not to focus on the throbbing pain in his groin. Instead, he focused on Becky, several hundred yards in front of him and heading towards the football field. Peter stepped up his pace to a jog, but felt a stitch in his side and was forced to slow down.

It was becoming increasingly clear to him that he was going to have to kill her. His hands shook at the thought, but his mind was steady. Becky Glidden was too dangerous for this time or any other.

The moment that thought crossed his brain, he wondered why she hadn't just jumped away into another time with Cassidy. He would be unable to find her if she did. He was glad she hadn't thought of it, but his mind continued to dwell on why she hadn't thought of it.

As he saw Becky and Cassidy enter the stadium, he picked up his pace to a full on run and quickly made up a lot of space between them. He ran in and made his way through the gate to the field and saw Becky push Cassidy to the ground. Cassidy sat up and Peter could see tears streaming down her face. Her crying had streaked her rainbow colored makeup down her face and Peter could see a dark strip of blood coming from her nose and mangling with the bright blues, oranges and pinks.

Becky kicked Cassidy back down and pulled a stiletto from a holster attached to her belt. Peter had no time to stop and mind move it away, so he continued to run at her full bore and ended up tackling her right as she was about to plunge the thin blade into Cassidy's heart. All three of them fell to the ground, but Peter was able to grab Becky and toss her further away from Cassidy.

Becky jumped up quickly and made her way for the girl again and Peter, who was still on the ground, kicked his legs at her gut and lifted her off the ground, throwing her back once more. He was able to get to his feet and saw flashing lights screaming down the road and heading towards the school.

"Peter, get the fuck out of my way," Becky screamed.

"I can't let you kill her or an innocent baby," Peter yelled back.

"Baby?" Cassidy asked.

Peter glanced at Cassidy, as if to ask if she was serious or not, and then back in time to see Becky plunge the stiletto into his neck. He crumpled to the ground instantly and his vision went cloudy. Cassidy screamed and Becky slapped her across the face, startling her into silence.

"You're pregnant, you stupid little cow," Becky yelled at Cassidy, towering over her with the knife. "That's my little bastard half brother in there." Becky tapped at Cassidy's crotch with the stiletto and Cassidy scrambled back a few feet. "My daddy slept with your slutty ass and if I don't kill you, he will. He'll go to jail and I'll grow up to become a drug addicted psycho."

Peter coughed up what seemed like a lake of blood and tried to speak.

"It doesn't have to be that way, Becky," he said, although very little of it came out intelligibly.

"What do you know, Peter?" she asked. "You're too afraid to take anything and live a decent life. Why do you think you never left this town anyway? You don't think you deserve it and you know what, you're right."

Peter blinked back tears at the pain of his very fatal wound and at the truth of Becky's remark. He deserved everything rotten that had ever happened to him and he stuck around to make sure nothing good ever came his way.

The police cars and fire trucks had made their way to the parking lot, but several of them had gone inside the school. It appeared as if none of them knew that anyone was on the football field.

Peter summoned every ounce of strength and focus he had left on trying to picture the gun on top of the school. He could see it and he tried to envision it in his hand, which he had stretched out, waiting for it. Becky cut Cassidy's belly and Cassidy gasped at the immense amount of pain.

Becky cut again and Peter growled in frustration, lifting himself inches off the ground, still waiting for the gun.

Becky raised the knife one more time, preparing to slash at Cassidy's throat.

"Goodbye, bitch," she said.

And then a gunshot went off.

Peter's world went black.

Epilogue

Halloween tragedy averted by actions of local hero
By Ken O'Donnell
kodonnell@cabotclarion.com

Living so close to Salem, Massachusetts, where the witch trials were held over 400 years ago, area residents know that this part of the state has seen its share of scary sights. A tragic event that featured a real life monster and would have produced yet another dark mark in the history of this county was prevented on Halloween by a former reporter for the Cabot Clarion, Peter Miller.

Miller, who stated that he had made a recent habit of walking around town at night while working on a novel, stumbled across an attempted murder of a high school student late Friday evening and got involved.

"I did what anybody else in this town would have done," Miller said from a hospital bed where he is recovering from a serious neck injury sustained in the attack. "This is a good place to live and we have to do everything we can to keep it that way."

The police have few details to provide, other than their discovery of the crime in progress was nothing short of a miracle.

"Several of our officers joined a group of firefighters responding to a fire alarm that had gone off inside the school," Detective Chris Leonard said in an exclusive interview early Saturday morning. "There was no one in the school, so we don't know how it went off, but we're damn glad it did. That girl is still alive because of it."

Leonard refused to identify the girl who is still recovering from her wounds at an undisclosed location.

The killer, a still unidentified woman armed with an illegal stiletto knife, was shot dead, but the officers either aren't sure who fired the fatal shot or aren't telling. Regardless, both Leonard and Miller agree that a terrible scene was narrowly avoided.

"That woman meant business," Miller said, adding that he had no idea who she was. "She'll be in my nightmares for awhile, I can tell you that much."

Leonard was quick to praise Miller's heroic efforts.

"We certainly don't recommend citizens trying to take the law into their own hands, but sometimes there really is no other choice," Leonard said. "I'm glad my old school chum Peter Miller has stuck around Cabot and has become the man he is today."

Clarion Publisher Jerry Jackson agreed with Leonard's comments and was quick to offer Miller a job at the paper as soon as he is well again. Miller has neither accepted or declined the position at this time.

"I want to thank Mr. Jackson for his support," Miller said. "I'll certainly consider it, but right now I just want to finish my novel. We'll see where I am when I've got that done."

While many bad things have occurred in our fair city over the years, it is good to know that there are still people willing to fight the good fight and protect the innocent. Miller's actions prove that there is a hero in all of us and that our time for heroic action can come at the most unlikely time and place.

June 5, 2012

Peter Miller sat on the lawn of Berrywood Park and listened to the Essex County Preservation Band perform a medley of ragtime tunes. He lay on a fuzzy blue Boston Red Sox blanket, propping his head up with his hands.

He gazed out at the little patch of ocean where several boats were moored, watching the sun set and set the water ablaze with orange and reddish hues.

He could breathe easy - had been able to breathe easy for years in fact. The wound in his neck healed rapidly and only left a small, circular scar. Only a few people who knew where to look for it, even noticed it.

"Daddy," a tiny voice called out and Peter turned his gaze to a little boy who's mouth was covered in a thin foam of chocolate. He was being trailed by a tall, beautiful woman in a straw hat and a classic white sun dress. They were returning from the ice cream stand and the woman, his wife, had a large chocolate shake in her hand. She took a sip.

"Hey, that's mine," he called out to her.

"I earned this," she said, flopping down next to Peter and patting a place for their son to sit.

Peter was blissfully happy watching his son bop his head to the music and lovingly stroking his wife's neck with a finger, cold from gripping the cup. Jeffrey may not have been his biological son, but he had been involved in his life since before he was born.

Peter had never consciously approached a relationship with Cassidy Samuels, now Miller, but their friendship organically made that leap about three months after her 20th birthday.

They had never had a run in again with Becky Glidden, despite the fact that she attended the same after school program as Jeffrey. Peter tried to avoid her when he picked up Jeffrey, but on several occasions she tried to strike up a conversation with him about horses.

"You should be a horse doctor and move far, far away from here," he told her once, looking up to see a disapproving look on the teacher's face. He shrugged, mouthed the word "sorry" and hustled Jeffrey out of the room and into the car.

Other than having the power to move things with his mind and leap around to other times and places, things he rarely did anymore, his life was pretty normal.

Still, there were times when he couldn't stop himself and neither he or Cassidy could find a reason to.

They annually made a quick trip to Woodstock and caught a little bit of the show.

www.ingramcontent.com/pod-product-compliance
Ingram Content Group UK Ltd.
Pitfield, Milton Keynes, MK11 3LW, UK
UKHW041958230426
12048UKWH00008B/404